RAY OF

HOPE

(Ray Series #2)

E. L. TODD

This is a work of fiction. All the characters and events portrayed in this novel are fictitious or used fictitiously. All rights reserved. No part of this book may be reproduced in any form or by any electronic or mechanical means, including information storage and retrieval systems, without written permission from the publisher or author, except in the case of a reviewer, who may quote brief passages in a review.

Fallen Publishing

Ray of Hope

Editing Services provided by Final-Edits.com

Copyright © 2017 by E. L. Todd All Rights Reserved

E. L. Todd

Chapter One

Rae

The second I walked in the door, Rex was up my ass.

"Damn, do you live there now?" He stood in the kitchen near the front door, clearly waiting for me to get home. He was in jeans and a sweater, ready to get out of the apartment and go downtown.

Zeke sat at the kitchen table behind him. He lifted up the beer he was drinking then rolled his eyes, admitting his best friend of twenty years was as much of a pain in the ass to him as he was to me.

"Rex, it's called a job." Safari came down the hallway, his tail wagging and excitement in his eyes. He greeted me much better than my brother ever did. "I know you don't know what that is since you sit on your ass all day and talk to a dog, but it's something us adults do every day." I kneeled down and kissed Safari before I scratched him behind the ears. "How's my favorite man?"

Rex watched us, his arms crossed over his chest. "I'm telling Ryker you said that."

"Go ahead." I patted Safari's head before I stood up. "I was sleeping with Safari long before I was sleeping with him." I headed down the hallway so I could stop this mind-numbing conversation. "I'm going to change."

"Ugh." Rex turned back to Zeke the moment I was gone. "It's like she wants me to throw up in her kitchen."

I went into my bedroom and changed into a pair of old jeans and a t-shirt. My favorite blue sweater hung on the edge of the bed, and I threw that on. It was covered with pieces of thick dog hair.

I looked at Safari with accusation.

He lowered his head in shame and wouldn't look at me.

"Safari, I told you not to lay on my clothes."

He whined.

I couldn't stay mad long when I looked at those mocha-colored eyes. He was such a sweetheart, the greatest dog a girl could ask for. "It's okay. Just don't do it again."

His ears perked up.

***

The bowling alley had been under reconstruction for the past month. The outside walls were given a new coat of paint, a brand new sign that said GROOVY BOWL was installed, and a large neon peace sign flashed in bright pink on the roof.

The three of us stopped on the sidewalk and admired it.

Rex stood in the middle, his arms over his chest and his neck craned so he could get a good look at the top of the building. "Damn, that looks pretty cool."

"It looks hip." Zeke took a few steps with his hands in his pockets, his t-shirt hugging his muscular chest as he moved. The veins in his forearms were obvious even from a few feet away. "I'd totally bowl here."

"Me too." Just a month ago, the place was the biggest dump in the city. Instead of looking like a cool place to hang out, it was the place to meet your dealer if you wanted an ounce of weed. Or it was a litter box for all the strays to pee. I had no understanding how Rex kept it open as long as he did. Maybe high school girls came to prey on him. His good looks were the only thing saving his ass. "It looks legit."

"Let's go inside." Rex pulled the keys from his pocket and unlocked the front doors. They were made of solid hard wood, looking like something from the 60's. An assortment of beads hung on the other side, and they brushed against us as we walked inside.

Rex got stuck, the long trail of beads wrapping around his neck. "What the hell?"

"On your neck." Zeke pointed to his right shoulder.

Rex turned around, only making it worse and getting another string stuck around his arm. "Agh!"

I dragged my hand down my face. "I can't believe this is happening…"

Rex twisted his arm and yanked but the beads bit into his forearm. "Help me!"

"Just unwrap them," Zeke said. "They're around your arm."

"How the hell are people supposed to get through this death trap?" Rex yanked and nearly pulled them out of the wall. "This is the stupidest idea ever. Did Rae think of this?" His face turned beet red, and when he tried to turn, he got even more wrapped up in the string until he could barely move. "I'm gonna die here."

I covered my face with both of my hands and took a deep breath so I wouldn't scream.

"Dude, are you gonna help me?" Rex stared at Zeke with a look of betrayal on his face. "Your best friend is dying and you don't even care?"

"You aren't dying." Zeke gave in and helped him pull the beads off. They were wrapped around both of his arms and his neck, and one by one, he pulled them away. When he was finally free, Rex took off so fast he tripped and fell onto the tile.

"I'm free!" He crawled back to his feet and brushed off his clothes like they were infected with a disease. "We need to get rid of those. They're a hazard."

"I can promise you, no one is going to get stuck in there." Not even a five-year-old would have struggled walking through. "You're just an idiot, Rex." Plain and simple.

"Whatever." Rex stuffed his hands in his pockets and eyed the beads like they were the gateway to hell. "Someone is gonna die because of those things." He turned to Zeke, the person he always looked at when he needed backup. "Right?"

Zeke cringed and shook his head slightly.

"Oh, come on." Rex stomped his foot like a child. "I'm not the only person that's going to happen to."

This conversation was making all of us dumber by the second. "Let's get a look at the rest of the place…"

Rex looked over his shoulder and eyed the beads like they might chase after him. He shivered noticeably and kept walking.

Zeke and I shared a look that clearly said, "Wow. That really just happened."

***

The bowling alley was a completely new place. There were no hints of the dump it once was. Everything had been remodeled, from the lanes themselves to the bathrooms. An arcade had been added, along with pool tables, a food cart, and a respectable bar.

Zeke hit the lights and the stereo, and the bowling alley came to life. The entire room was dimmed until it was nearly black then the lanes popped with the groovy lights. Images of peace signs and old Volkswagens moved across the walls, a brilliant light show. A popular Beatles song played on the sound system, taking us back in time.

Rex eyed everything in awe, finally recovered from his near-death experience. "This place is so fucking sick. I can't believe it."

"I can't either." Zeke stood beside him and took in everything. "This place is going to be a hit. I can tell."

Zeke and I put a lot of money down for this place, and anyone would have told me it was a stupid idea but I didn't have any regrets. Even if it didn't work out, it was okay. I regretted the things I didn't do more than the things I actually did do. I would rather take a chance and hope Rex succeeded than accept his immediate failure. "It's perfect." Pride rushed through me as I stared at the transformation. I could already picture families coming here every Sunday night as a tradition.

Rex turned in a circle and examined everything. "You know what? We're missing something..."

Zeke met his look like he knew exactly what he was doing. "The dancers?"

"Yep." Rex snapped his fingers. "I really think that would pull everything together."

I rolled my eyes. "Maybe they can dance under a string of beads."

Rex's face immediately contorted into a look of pure torture. "That's not funny. They could die."

I crossed my arms over my chest and shook my head. "Rex, they wouldn't die."

"I almost did!" He pointed to the entrance. "Those things have got to go. Otherwise, we're going to have an arson case on our hands."

Zeke and I both exchanged a look when neither of us understood what he meant.

Zeke was the one who addressed it. "Arson?"

"You know, when someone is murdered." Rex said it with such confidence it seemed like it could be true.

"Rex, arson is when you set property on fire." Why was I even bothering explaining this to him?

"No, it's not," Rex said. "I learned about it at college."

"You mean traffic school?" Zeke asked without rolling his eyes. "Sorry, man. That's not college."

"And if they said that, they're the worst traffic school in the country." And I should be scared next time I was on the road.

"I know you brainiacs are just trying to mess with me," Rex said. "And I'm not falling for it."

"Yeah…we're trying to mess with you." If he wanted to go out and tell someone murder was called arson, then he could be my guest. Maybe it would stop him from bringing those strange women back to the apartment.

"Guess we didn't fool you." Zeke looked at me, his jaw tensed and his lips pressed tightly together as he suppressed a laugh.

"I guess the joke's on us." Sometimes it was better to let Rex think whatever he wanted. When it came around and bit him in the ass, it was always fun to watch. "Should we get something to eat?"

"Yeah," Rex said. "I'm starving."

"Me too." Zeke hit the lights and we walked back to the entrance.

Rex stopped before the beads, his feet planted firmly on the carpet. He eyed them like they were made from venomous snakes.

Zeke and I shared a look.

"You know what..." Rex took three steps backward. "I'm going to go out the back way."

"You've got to be kidding me." He was going to come to work and leave every day through the back entrance?

Rex had already turned around and was headed to the opposite end of the bowling alley.

Now that he was gone, Zeke laughed. "Just let him be. He'll conquer his fear someday."

"How are you his best friend?" Zeke was smart, funny, and he wasn't an annoying pain in the ass.

He shrugged. "I consider it community service."

I smiled because it was a great answer. "Then I've been doing community service my whole life."

***

I took Safari outside then hopped in the shower. I was supposed to be at Ryker's an hour ago but we were at the bowling alley a lot longer than I expected. Plus, we got hot wings and that took another thirty minutes. Since I was starving, I didn't skip out.

After I finished getting dressed, my phone lit up.

Why is my bed empty and cold? Ryker's irritated voice came through the text message.

Maybe you need a dog. Oh, I loved being a smartass.

Maybe I need to chain you to the headboard.

That didn't sound so bad. *Nah, I'd get hungry. And you know I pee around the clock.*

I'd give you bathroom privileges.

How generous. This could go on all night so I needed to wrap it up. *I'm heading out now. See you soon.*

Run.

I shoved my phone into my pocket and gave Safari a kiss.

Like every night I slept at Ryker's, he looked at me like I was the worst parent in the world. He gave me a guilt trip with those mocha-colored eyes. When he released a quiet whine, he just made it worse.

"I'll be back tomorrow."

He bowed his head then lay on the ground, looking like the most depressed dog in existence.

I'd been staying at Ryker's a lot lately, at least half of the week, and Safari slept alone in my room. He didn't sleep with Rex because he preferred my bed, probably because it smelled like me. Thinking about that made me feel even worse. I pulled out my phone and texted him. *Don't get mad, alright?*

Too late.

I'm gonna stay here tonight.

I'll break down that door.

I knew he wasn't kidding. *Sorry...*

What's the hold up?

When I told him it was my dog, he would be more annoyed. *Safari. I haven't been sleeping here and he's so miserable.*

You'd rather sleep with a dog than me? I could hear the sarcasm through the words.

Not rather. I feel like I've been abandoning him.

He's a dog.

So are you. I didn't see too many differences.

He ignored the jab. *Then I'll sleep over there.*

I didn't want that either. *I don't want you staying here too often. It's just weird with my brother next door.*

Are you dating me? Or your brother and your dog?

Keep it up and I won't be dating either of you.

The dots disappeared and he went radio silent.

Yep. He was super pissed now. I understood his frustration, but he also needed to understand he wasn't the only person in my life. I had a lot of friends and a brother who needed me right now. Ryker was used to getting what he wanted at the drop of a hat, and he never got his way with me. *Good night.* I tossed the phone on the bed then looked at Safari. "Thanks to you, I'm not getting any tonight."

Safari somehow knew I was staying home, and he rose on his hind legs and placed his paws on my chest. His tail wagged and his tongue popped out of his mouth and jiggled back and forth. Whines of happiness came from his large mouth.

"But at least I'll have someone to cuddle with." I gave him a good rub down and then a hug, knowing I loved my dog as much as I loved everyone else in my life. I saved him from traffic in the road, but he saved me too.

***

"I thought you were going to Ryker's?" Rex sat on the couch with a beer on his thigh. A game was on but he was only partially watching it. His elbow was propped on the armrest and he rested his temple against his open palm. With sagged shoulders and an attitude of misery, he looked depressed.

I stood at the opposite end of the couch, Safari at my heels. "I decided to stay with Safari. I've been neglecting him."

Rex didn't make a jab like he normally would. He sat there in complete silence.

I knew something was up. "Everything alright?"

"Yeah." He drank his beer to mask his unease at the question.

Something was definitely wrong. "I know something is on your mind. So save me the fishing trip and just tell me."

He put his beer on the coffee table and leaned forward. "I'm just worried about tomorrow."

"The grand opening?" I sat down, keeping several feet between us.

"Yeah…"

"What's there to worry about? Everything is ready to go. You just have to unlock the doors."

"What if no one shows up?"

Zeke and I had done extensive marketing for this bowling alley, everything from taking out ads in the paper, to handing out flyers and hitting up people on Facebook. I wasn't worried it would be a soft opening. I knew it would be a hit. "Rex, it'll be fine."

"But what if it's not?"

"If it's not, we'll figure something out. Don't worry about it."

He shook his head like I didn't understand something. "I don't care if the bowling alley goes under and I lose the money I invested. That's a destiny I accepted a long time ago. But I don't want to lose the money you guys put into it. That's what I'm worried about."

"Not gonna happen, Rex."

"But you don't know that."

"I do." I wasn't a businessman, but I knew this would be a success.

"How?"

"I just do. And even if it isn't, Zeke and I will be fine. Neither one of us put all our cash into this."

"That doesn't matter." His voice thickened, turning angry. "You guys worked your asses off for that cash. Zeke already opened his own office and took a risk. You had to pay back student loans. I don't want to blow your hard earned cash."

Nothing I said was going to make him feel better. "No matter what happens, worrying about it isn't going to change anything. And no matter what happens, we have our health, food on the table, and somewhere to live. Money is just money, Rex. Remember the important things in life." I remember when Rex and I had nowhere to live. He couldn't hold down a job and we struggled for a while. We were lucky when Zeke took us in until Rex could find his footing.

He didn't have a comeback when I put everything in perspective.

"Just chill, alright? Drink more beer. Eat more food."

He finally released a chuckle. "You act like I'm a mindless caveman."

"Because you are."

He chuckled again. "I guess I can be."

"I just know—"

A knock sounded on the door and Safari immediately barked at the intrusion. Like the watchdog he was, he went to the front door to investigate who the intruder was.

"Zeke?" I asked.

He shrugged. "I don't think so."

I went to the door and spotted Ryker through the peephole. Both of my eyebrows shot up, and I opened the door. "Uh, hi."

After Safari cleared Ryker, he walked away and returned to the living room with Rex.

"Hi." He wore his sweatpants and sneakers with a gray hoodie. Even dressed down in lounge wear, he looked unbelievable. He could walk into a bar and pick up any woman he wanted.

"Everything alright?" When he didn't text me back, I assumed he was in a bad mood. But I figured it would blow over by the following morning.

"I'm picking you up. Go grab your stuff."

"I said I was staying with Safari."

"And you are. Bring him along."

My eyebrow rose. "You want a big, hairy dog in your palace?"

He shrugged. "I know you two come as a pair. Besides, your hair gets in all my sinks and drains anyway. Not much different."

Now my eyes narrowed.

The corner of his mouth rose in a smile. "Grab Safari and let's go."

There's nothing I wanted more but I knew I shouldn't leave Rex. "I'd love to but I really should stay here..." I leaned forward and pressed my mouth to his ear. "Rex is really stressed about the grand opening tomorrow." I pulled away.

He was irritated all over again but he didn't make an argument. "I get it."

"I'm sorry..."

Rex came to the door and nodded to Ryker. "What's up, man?"

"Just wanted to stop by and see Rae."

Rex grabbed another beer from the fridge. "Are you going to his place?" His question was directed at me.

"No," I said quickly. "He just came to say goodnight."

Rex wasn't buying it because he wasn't as stupid as I claimed he was. "I don't know what's going on here, but I have a feeling it has something to do with me."

Ryker spilled the beans. "I wanted to take both her and Safari back to my place, but she wants to stay here with you, which I understand."

Rex was about to drink his beer but lowered the bottle again. "Rae, I'm fine. Go."

"I really don't mind staying—"

"Dude, I'm okay. You put it all in perspective for me." He patted me on the shoulder. "Go live your life and stop being a loser that hangs out with her brother and dog too much."

Ryker nodded. "I couldn't have said it better myself." His eyes turned to me, and his irritation was palpable.

"I'll see you at the opening tomorrow." Rex walked into the living room and disappeared from the entryway.

Ryker looked at me with victory in his eyes. "Grab you bag and let's go."

Safari folded his ears when he thought Ryker was taking me away.

"Safari, you're coming too." Ryker patted his thigh and whistled. "Come on, boy."

Safari raced out the door and nearly knocked Ryker to the floor.

Ryker chuckled as he righted himself. "I don't think I've ever seen him that excited."

"Me neither."

***

Ryker shut the bedroom door so we could have some privacy from my spoiled dog. He pulled his shirt over his head then dropped his sweats. He wasn't wearing boxers underneath so his cock popped out, hard and ready to go even though we just walked inside.

"Damn, you're hard up, huh?"

"What gave me away?" He walked toward me, his cock long and proud. He sat at the foot of the bed then leaned back and pulled the pillows under his head. His dick lay against his stomach, and without saying anything, he told me what he wanted.

"Are you trying to tell me something?"

"Yep." He wrapped his hand around his shaft and slowly moved up and down. "I've been thinking about that pretty mouth all day. And since you were such a pain in the ass for the past two hours, you owe me."

"I owe you?" I forced an attitude even though I didn't have one. I'd gladly suck his dick without him asking. His cock was absolutely beautiful and did the most amazing things to my body. I didn't mind cherishing it with my tongue.

"Yep. But when you're done, I'll owe you." He gave me a smoldering look. "Think about it that way."

"That does sound tempting..." I removed my sweater and jeans, taking my time as I stripped down to my bra and panties. His eyes were glued to my frame, and he watched me with a gaze so hot it burned my skin. I watched him swallow the lump in his throat. When his cock twitched, I knew he liked the mini strip tease I just gave him. I unhooked my bra and let it fall to the hardwood floor with a quiet thud. Then I turned around so my ass was in his face. Slowly, I pulled my panties over my ass and down my thighs, exposing every inch slowly, dragging it out as long as possible. When I reached my thighs and exposed my slick folds, I heard him moan from behind me.

I smirked then kicked my black thong away. I kneeled between his thighs, my tits touching his balls as they hung over the edge. They were warm and tight, anxious to release the seed he'd been building up all day.

Ryker watched me, his eyes so dark they were nearly black. His hand snaked up my shoulder until it got a fist full of hair. His signature move was to grab me by the back of the neck, like a predator watching over prey. He grabbed his cock by the base and lifted his head until it rubbed against my lips like Chap Stick. "Now I'm not sure if I want to fuck your mouth or your pussy."

"Who says you can't do both?" I pressed my lips to the tip of his cock and gave him a wet kiss, absorbing the bead of lubricant his body produced.

He moaned under his breath, watching me with pure fascination.

I grabbed his base and moved his hand out of the way then licked the upper part of his shaft like a lollipop. I took my time, dragging my tongue slowly around the head of his cock where he was most sensitive. "Mmm…"

He gripped my hair tighter, gently pulling on my scalp. "You like that, sweetheart?"

"No. I love it." I opened my mouth and pushed his cock to the back of my throat. I could only take half of him because he was too long. If I pushed any farther, I would engage my gag reflex—and that wasn't sexy. My hand massaged his balls as I moved him in and out of my throat.

Ryker placed both hands behind his head and watched me, enjoying the show as much as the experience. His cock was unnaturally hard in my mouth because he enjoyed it so much. His hips moved slowly, rocking himself into me. "Fuck, you give amazing head."

I pulled his cock out of my mouth. "Only when I really enjoy it." I gave him a dark look with my eyes before I kept going.

"You like sucking my dick, sweetheart?"

"Oh yeah."

His hand returned to the back of my hair. "I want this to last forever, but I really want to fuck you."

I kept going, challenging him to stop me.

He didn't. He continued to guide my mouth up and down his length. He pushed me farther than I wanted to go by a few centimeters but I didn't gag. Sweat formed on his chest and his breathing increased. His cock twitched in my mouth, and I knew he was approaching his threshold.

I loved pleasing him as much as he loved being pleased. His eyes darkened and somehow turned lifeless because his mind was high in the clouds. All rationale had disappeared as he ascended into the realm of complete pleasure. The desperation to come filled him, and he fought with little restraint. "It's coming."

"Give it to me."

He took a deep breath and pulled me down his length, releasing deep in the back of my throat. "Fuck…" His fingers dug into the back of my neck and his hips thrust slightly, making sure I got every drop.

I sucked everything off his tip before I pulled him out of my mouth. Semi-hard, his cock landed against his stomach with a gentle tap. He was soaked in my saliva and his balls loosened after the explosion. "Whenever you're ready." I crawled up the bed and laid my head on the pillows. I spread my legs and waited for him.

He didn't hesitate before he crawled up the bed and pressed his face between my legs. His tongue darted out and began the intense pleasure session. He sucked me aggressively, wanting to give me head that rivaled the kind I just gave him.

I stared down at him with my fingers deep in his hair. My thighs were spread wide apart, and I enjoyed the scorching heat he just gave me. I didn't think about all the women who'd been in this bed before I came along. I just thought about the magic we were making in that moment. No man had ever made me feel so satisfied. Ryker never left me hanging, and he worked to make every experience better than the last. He would never know how much I appreciated that.

"Come, sweetheart." His eyes looked into mine as he licked my clit hard.

His precise touch and the desire in his eyes made my body obey his command. My fingers dug into his scalp, and I felt my hips contract automatically as the orgasm hit me like a freight train. "Oh god…"

He sucked me harder, making it hit me hard and long.

"Yes…yes."

***

I washed my face and got ready for bed even though it was early morning. I pulled on one of his t-shirts and a new pair of panties since my other pair was soaked. Then I opened the bedroom door and let Safari inside. "Ready for bed, Safari?"

He immediately jumped on the bed and made himself at home.

Ryker lay in bed with his hands behind his head. He eyed Safari with an amused expression. "Just don't pee on anything, alright?"

"He won't." I rubbed my dog's head and gave him a kiss. "He's a good boy."

Ryker watched our interaction. "Sometimes I wonder if you like him more than me."

"I do." I said it without shame. "He's been my best friend for years. He can't be replaced that easily."

"I guess I'll have to step it up."

"Really have to step it up." I turned off the bedside lamp and got into bed.

Ryker immediately snuggled with me, his arm hooked around my waist. His gentle breaths fell on the back of my neck, and his concrete chest pressed into my back. With every breath, his chest pushed against me, reminding me he was real and not just a dream.

"Thanks for letting Safari stay here."

"I'll bend over backwards to be with you, Rae. But I think you already knew that."

Ray of Hope

Chapter Two

Rae

The second the doors were open, it was packed.

Families and friends scattered throughout Groovy Bowl. Some hit the lanes right away with their teams and began to bowl. The younger crowd hit the arcade and the pizzeria while the parents went to the small bar tucked in the corner.

I wasn't the least bit surprised.

"Dude, we actually have customers." Rex stood in a Groovy Bowl t-shirt. It was a tie-dyed shirt with a bowling ball in the center. "People really came."

"Of course they did." Jessie was dressed like a beauty queen like always, her hair straight and designer jeans tight on her hips. "Just from the outside, this place looks awesome. How else would people want to spend their Saturday?"

"It's so cool." Kayden looked at the place in complete awe. Of everyone in the group, she seemed to be the most impressed. "Can I buy a t-shirt?"

"You can't buy one," Rex said. "But I'll give it to you."

"Come on, let me buy one," she pressed.

"No," Rex argued. "Your money is no good here." He walked off to get the t-shirt from behind the counter.

Zeke turned to me. "Looks like we did it."

"I think it's safe to say this place is gonna be around for a long time." The crowd would thin out in a few weeks, but after a big opening like this, customers would be steady. Zeke and I came up with an idea to give out awards to the people who bowled the best for each month, and we expected that would bring even more people in.

"Now Rex can calm the hell down."

"And move out." That was the part I was most excited about. Ryker could stay at my place and make my life easier. He could walk into work whenever he wanted, but I had to be there at the same time every day. When I stayed at his place, I had to get up even earlier just to get ready. And I wasn't a morning person to begin with. Besides, Safari preferred to stay in the apartment. He made it work at Ryker's last night, but I knew he wasn't comfortable there.

Zeke chuckled. "You can finally get your life back. What are you going to do when he's gone?"

"Sterilize the place."

He laughed. "You're going to have to use some serious bleach. Some stains won't come out."

"Maybe I'll just move."

"Now you're thinking outside the box."

"Should we get some pizza?" Jessie asked. "I'm hungry."

"Me too." Kayden rubbed her stomach like she hadn't eaten in days.

"Sounds like a plan." Just when we turned to walk to the pizzeria, Rex returned with a handful of t-shirts. He handed them out.

I held mine up to my chest. "These are so cute."

Zeke took off his shirt, showing off his powerful pecs and washboard abs.

Jessie whistled. "Damn."

"Wow," Kayden said. "Someone overuses their gym membership."

Zeke smiled as he pulled on the Groovy Bowl t-shirt. He was too humble to say anything, but his smug grin said he appreciated the compliments. "It's good material. Really soft."

"Everything feels soft when you're made of concrete," Jessie said.

Zeke smiled again.

Rex narrowed his eyes like he felt left out. "Hey, I've got a nice physique too."

"Prove it," Jessie said.

"Yeah." Kayden's eyes were wide like Christmas ornaments on a tree. "Prove it right now."

I held up my hand. "Please don't. It's been such a good day, and we wouldn't want to ruin it by throwing up on the new tile."

Rex ignored me and took off his shirt anyway.

Jessie whistled. "Damn...I'm not sure who has the nicer body."

Rex flexed a bicep, showing his prominent muscles and his lean build. "It's not even a close contest, ladies."

Kayden continued to stare at him, her jaw open.

"Zeke definitely has the better bod." There was no contest in my eyes.

Zeke turned to me then nudged me in the side. "Like what you see, huh?"

"A lot better than Mr. Albino over there."

"Hey," Rex snapped. "It's been raining a lot lately."

"Zeke isn't pale as snow," I argued. "And he lives in the same city." Zeke had a tan look to him, but I didn't know where it came from. I knew he did a lot of biking, but I couldn't picture him doing it shirtless.

"He's a dermatologist," Rex snapped. "He probably put some chemicals on to make his skin look like that."

"Yeah," Zeke deadpanned. "It's called vitamin D."

"Where do you get that?" Rex asked. "Do they have it at Rite-Aid?"

Unanimously, we all turned to the pizza parlor. "Let's get some lunch," I said. "I'm burning way too many calories trying to understand that dipshit."

***

Rex showed the girls the bar, the place they were most interested in seeing. Zeke and I ate more than everyone else so we were always the two left behind. I took another slice and went to town on it, trying not to think about the six mile run I'd have to do tomorrow to make up for this evening. I sighed when I realized how much my feet would hurt halfway through the run.

Zeke sipped his soda, his eyes on me.

"Seeing anyone?" He mentioned he had a hookup not too long ago. Maybe he did a back-to-back.

"I went out with this woman last night."

"How'd that go?"

"It was okay." He wiped his greasy fingers on a napkin. "I don't think I'll see her again."

"Why not?"

He shrugged. "Didn't feel anything."

"Did you sleep with her?" I knew I could ask him questions like that at point blank. He did the same to me.

"Yeah." He didn't show any guilt for his one-night stand. "It was good, but I don't know…just not interested."

Zeke was the perfect catch. He was sweet and thoughtful, and he was honest and loyal. Someday, he would make the perfect husband and father. Whoever ended up with him was one of the luckiest women on the planet. "You'll find the right girl. She's out there somewhere…"

He quickly averted his gaze and drank his soda. "Yeah…I'm sure I will."

"It sounds like you aren't really looking for something serious."

"I'm not." He sipped his soda again, chugging it like water. "Just playing the field right now. I've been going to the bars after work and have been getting lucky with the numbers."

"It's not luck," I said with a serious expression. "You're a perfect ten, Zeke."

He set his soda down and stared at me—hard. "You really think so?"

"Hell yeah, I do." Even if I were gay, I would still think it. "When you don't call those women the next day, they're probably so disappointed. Trust me on that."

He nodded slightly like he didn't know what else to do. "How's it going with Ryker?"

"Good." We'd spent the last month doing the same routine. Sometimes we went out to dinner, but most of the time, we just went to his place and hooked up. I didn't mind because the sex was awesome, but I was starting to worry our relationship was too superficial.

"Sounds like there's more to the story."

"Why do you say that?"

"Because your answer is one word. You usually talk more than that." He pushed his empty plate to the side and rested his elbows on the table.

"I guess…I'm a little concerned about it."

"Because?"

"There's a one-word question."

His smile deepened. "Don't be a smartass. Just answer the question."

"I'm concerned because we don't do much talking." I didn't elaborate on that part because Zeke could fill in the dots. "I know him, but I don't really know him. It seems like he likes me, and I believe he does, but then I also wonder where this is really going. But it's way too soon to ask that kind of question."

Zeke remained silent, being a good listener.

"So...I don't know."

"Maybe this is just a fling. Maybe it's supposed to run its course and you guys are supposed to go your separate ways. There's nothing wrong with that."

"Yeah, but that's exactly what I was trying to avoid."

Zeke knew exactly why so he didn't say anything.

"I just don't want to get my heart broken again. It sucks." I sighed when I remembered how excruciating it was.

"He can't break your heart unless you allow him to. So don't let him."

I laughed in a sarcastic way. "You make it sound so easy."

"I also think if you have the mindset that this relationship is going to fail, then it probably will." He shrugged like he didn't know what else to say. "So maybe you need to make some changes."

"Like?"

"Try getting to know him better. More dates and less sex."

"But I don't want less sex…" It was amazing, the best I'd ever had.

Zeke would normally laugh at that comment but this time he didn't. "Or you could tell him about your concerns."

"Ryker isn't the type of guy who does serious conversations like this…"

"Then maybe he isn't the right guy for you. Relationships are about communication. If you can't talk, then you'll never understand each other." Zeke was much wiser than me, probably because he was older and smarter. When he said something, it was usually true.

"You have a point."

He shrugged again. "Do what you want. I'm sure you'll make the right decision."

"Yeah, I hope so."

His eyes turned to the TV in the corner. "Mariners are up."

I glanced over my shoulder and saw the score. "Hell yeah. I knew today was going to be a great day." I turned back to him and grabbed another slice.

Zeke let a smile form on his lips.

"What? Are you judging me?"

"Absolutely not. I just think it's interesting you eat so much but never gain weight."

"Ha." I laughed because it was totally absurd. "Believe me, I do. It goes straight to my thighs. That's why I never wear shorts."

"I thought that was because you're always cold."

"Nope. Now you know the real reason."

"Your legs are fine, Rae. I look at them every day."

"But you don't *really* look at them."

He turned his eyes back to the TV. "Thinking of buying a house soon?"

"Now that Rex will be able to pay us back within a year, I think I'll wait. But I do want something. I really like your neighborhood."

He nodded. "It's quiet. I like it."

It was a luxurious neighborhood I could never afford, but I loved to admire it. Zeke's house was way too big for just a single person, but it suited him so well. When he got married and had kids, it would be the perfect place to raise a family. Sometimes I was jealous, but then I remembered how hard he worked for everything he had, and I'd realize I had no right to be jealous. If I wanted the things he had, I needed to work harder. "I'll start seriously looking soon. The market is good right now, so I should jump on it."

"True. Let me know if you need any help. I learned a lot from my realtor."

"Thanks. I'll probably need all the help I can get."

"Nah. You're a lot smarter than you give yourself credit for. In fact, you're one of the smartest people I know."

I appreciated that Zeke never said I was one of the "smartest women he knew." Most people said things like that, like they were impressed with what I accomplished with the burden between my legs. Zeke always treated me like an equal, and he didn't view me the same way other people did. "Thanks. But I'm not as smart as you."

"I'm really not as smart as people claim I am."

"You're just being humble."

He shook his head. "I accidentally drove away with my gas pump still attached to the car. Not so much now, huh?" He grinned from ear to ear at the memory.

"When did that happen?"

"Like a year ago. I never told anyone because I knew I would be teased forever."

"How much did it cost to repair it?"

"A few thousand bucks. It sucked."

I didn't laugh because he seemed truly embarrassed about it even though it really was funny. "Now I have some dirt on you."

"And I have a lot of dirt on you I can spill to Ryker."

"Damn…" He got me.

He chuckled then grabbed his soda again. "I'm not an opponent you want to mess with, Rae."

I knew that all too well.

Rex and the girls came back to the table with their beers and cosmos.

"Where's ours?" Zeke asked.

"I'm not your boyfriend," Rex barked. "Get your own."

"But he's your investor," I reminded him. "As am I."

"Just because you're my investor doesn't mean I have to kiss your ass." Rex sat down with his drink, Kayden beside him.

Zeke and I both shot him the stink eye, giving him a silent guilt trip until he got his ass out of his seat.

Rex finally broke under our glares and got up. "Fine. Two beers are on the way."

Chapter Three

Rae

Ryker texted me. *Want to come over?*

He went straight for the kill, like always. *How about we go to dinner?*

I can order a pizza.

I've been wanting to try that new Chinese place next to my apartment. Besides, you always say you're going to order a pizza but never do.

I really will this time. It'll be ready when you get here.

No thanks. Pick me up at 7 if you want to go to that Chinese place.

There was a long pause without the three dots. After about a minute, they appeared. *See you soon.*

I smiled in triumph.

***

Ryker picked me up and drove us to the Chinese place. We walked inside and got a table with a white tablecloth and a candle sitting in the center. Ryker didn't say much. He stared at his menu until he decided what he wanted. Then he put it down and stared at me instead.

"How was your day?" I didn't see him at work unless he came down to the lab, which wasn't very often. Jenny worked the same shift, and if she saw him too often, she would get suspicious. I didn't want anyone at work to know we were seeing each other because people would immediately turn their noses up at me—especially Jenny.

"Boring." He always gave the same answer in regards to his time in the office.

"That's it?"

"Pretty much. I do a bunch of paperwork all day, take lunch, and then do more paperwork until three o' clock comes around. It's not as exciting as all the scientific discoveries you make down there in the bunker."

"Unfortunately, I haven't made any scientific discoveries yet."

"Give it time. How was your day?"

"I got a lot done. I finished one trial of my experiment and got good results. But now I need to repeat it two more times."

"Because…?"

"For an experiment to be valid, it must be replicated with the same results."

"But you aren't publishing a paper in the Yale Journal of Biology."

I wish I were. "No, but to ask for the funding to continue my project, I want to be completely certain of my data."

He nodded. "My dad wasn't kidding about you. Said you were one of the best workers at the company."

Mr. Price was a good man, and I would never forget him. "How's he doing?"

Ryker paused before he answered. "Good. Plays golf." He never talked about his father much even though we both knew him in different ways.

Sometimes, I got the impression he didn't care for his father, like he was resentful for being forced to take over the company when he stepped down. I wanted to ask but I suspected the intrusion wouldn't be appreciated.

"What were you doing in New York before you came here?" I realized I didn't know that either. I jumped into bed with him because he had a pretty face and a pretty body. Those were the only prerequisites I cared about.

"I was living in my penthouse near the park."

That didn't answer my question at all. I didn't ask where he was living. "Where did you work?"

"I didn't."

"Oh..." Then what did he do all day? Did he live off his father's cash?

"My dad gave me a trust, and I invested it all into stocks, real estate, and bonds. I've been living off the interest ever since." He answered the question even though I never asked it. He could see it on the tip of my tongue. "I spent my time playing video games, traveling, and enjoying the night life."

I understood what that last part meant. "I understand why you were so miserable coming here."

"When my dad told me to take over the company, I wasn't happy. But I didn't have a choice. Besides, if I hadn't come here, I wouldn't have met you." He looked at me with a gaze mixed with lust and sincerity. "So it worked out in the end."

It was a sweet thing to say, and I absorbed it through my skin to cherish as a memory. "I guess it did."

"I admit I'm fond of the weather here. Pretty mild all year round. In New York, it's either freezing cold or humid as hell. Have you been?"

"No." I'd never left Washington.

"I'll take you sometime. I think you'd like it."

"I'd love to see it at some point."

"Have any vacation time free in the near future?"

"I get three weeks every year and haven't use it yet. So we're set."

"I'll give you more than three weeks. You can take as many as you want."

It was a nice offer, but I wouldn't take it. "I respect your company too much to take advantage of you. I'm grateful for everything COLLECT has given me, and I don't want to be treated differently just because I'm seeing you. I hope you accept that and don't take that offensively."

Ryker took in my words without a single reaction. "If that's what you want, I understand."

"Thank you." I thought he might push me on the subject but he backed off.

Ryker became quiet again, but his eyes lingered on my face. His lustful thoughts were obvious. I could see an image of us fucking on his bed in the gloss of his eyes. Did he ever think about anything else?

We ordered our food and that broke up the tension for a few moments before it settled on the table once more. The more I tried to talk to him, get to know him, the tenser it became. Ryker was the strong and silent type. He was content saying nothing all night long. If I didn't say anything, neither would he.

"I want to ask you something."

He cocked his head slightly, his face painfully handsome. "I'm all ears."

"Does it bother you that we don't talk very much?"

"I don't understand your question. I see you almost every day."

"I know we see each other. But we don't really know each other. I feel like the only time we connect is when we're screwing."

"Isn't that the most important connection?" One of his eyebrows rose, and even when he was confused he was still sexy.

"It's important, yes. But all we do is go to your house and have sex. We never go out or do anything."

"What are we doing now?" he asked like a smartass.

"Because I forced your hand." And he didn't make it easy.

He sighed quietly, not hiding his irritation. "Rae, I'm confused. Are you telling me I'm not doing enough for you? Because I've done more for you than I've done for anyone else. I admit I'm a little closed off, but I don't have much to say. That's who I am. Always have been and always will be. I thought we were both happy but it sounds like you aren't. If that's the case, then do you still want to do this?"

"Of course." Being with him wasn't the issue. "I just…get concerned we're doing something wrong."

"If you have certain expectations of how this should be, then yeah, it'll always feel wrong. I like having you at my apartment because I get to enjoy you in private. It's not just about sex. It's about touching you and kissing you. It's about being with you in the most intimate way possible. I'm not trying to hide you, and I don't only want sex. I do want more. When we're out in public, I have to hold myself back. I can't touch you when I feel like it. I can't kiss you when I feel like it. You're overthinking this."

"Maybe I am…"

"No, you are."

"I just feel like I can't talk to you the way I talk to my friends. With them, we tell each other everything. But with us, we don't really share much."

He didn't blink as he stared me down. "Because I'm not your friend, Rae. Our relationship is different than what you have with them—in a good way. We're physical and romantic. We connect in a different way—a physical way."

Maybe he was right. Maybe I was trying to find an excuse to end this relationship before it ended on its own. I knew I was falling for him. Every single day, I was a little deeper in the hole. Every kiss, every touch, and every time we had sex was sucking me further in. I didn't know what it was about Ryker that made me feel this way. Sometimes I thought he was too good to be true. And sometimes I feared he was with me for the wrong reasons—because I stood up to him, unlike all the others.

"So, are we okay?"

His voice brought me back to the conversation. "Yeah."

"Are you sure?" He leaned over the table and lowered his voice.

"Yes."

"Would you be pissed if I got this food to go so I can eat it off you?"

"Chinese food isn't very sexy…"

He lowered his voice even more. "Believe me, I can make it sexy."

***

The phone rang in the lab and Jenny answered. "Hello? Yeah, she's right here." She set the receiver on the counter. "Rae, it's for you."

"Who is it?"

"Kayden."

"Cool." I ripped off my gloves and tossed them in the safety box before I grabbed the phone. "Hey, girl. What's up?"

"Are you busy right now?"

"Not really. I just harvested my specimens and transferred them to the petri dishes. Then I need to incubate—"

"You know I don't understand that mumbo jumbo."

"And you know I don't know what mumbo jumbo means. So what's up?"

"I was wondering if Ryker has any single friends you could hook me up with. He's gorgeous so maybe he knows other gorgeous guys."

Kayden didn't chase after guys, and she didn't show much interest in the dating world. Maybe she was finally out of her funk and realized she needed to get laid. "Where's this coming from?"

"I guess seeing you with Ryker makes me miss dating."

And it would make any girl miss good sex. "I can ask him."

"Thanks. That would be great. And please don't set me up with a weirdo like how Jess did to you."

"You mean the firefighter with the curious tongue?"

"Yeah. Yuck."

"I'd never do that to one of my girls. Not sure what Jess's problem was."

"She probably didn't know. So make sure you do your research for me."

"I will. Talk to you later."

"Bye. Love you."

"Love you too." I hung up.

"You tell your friends you love them when you get off the phone?"

"Yeah." Some people might think it's weird but I didn't. "We could all use more love in the world."

Jenny made a strange face then walked away.

She probably thought I was a lesbian. But whatever. It was better than her thinking I was sleeping with Ryker.

***

I called Ryker on the cab drive home.

"Hey, sweetheart. I was just thinking about you."

"Are your hands in your pants?" I glanced at the driver and didn't care if he could hear me. He'd probably overheard worse conversations.

He chuckled into the phone. "No. But they will be soon unless you come over."

"You always want me over there."

"Can you blame me? Look at you."

I smiled unwillingly and saw my reflection in the rearview mirror. I looked like a stupid love struck teenager. "I was actually calling for something else."

"You want me to go over there? I can do that. When is Rex moving out, by the way?"

"Not soon enough." I ignored the first question. "Kayden wants to know if you have any hot friends you can hook her up with."

"I wouldn't know if I had hot friends."

"Don't be annoying," I said. "It's not rocket science to know if someone of the same sex is attractive."

"It's not. But I'm also not gay."

"This masculine bullshit is annoying. I know Kayden and Jess are both damn fine, and I'm totally straight."

"My cock agrees with you on that part."

I paused over the line.

"About you being straight," he clarified. "Your friends are pretty, but I've never gotten hard for either one of them."

At least that cured the awkwardness.

"I'll see what I can do. I have a few local friends. I'll ask around."

"Thanks."

"She can't find a guy on her own? I'm surprised."

"She's gorgeous but shy."

"Honestly, just have her walk into a bar in a tight skirt, and she'll have her pick of the crop. Any woman can do it if they give off the right vibe."

"I think she's looking for someone that checks out."

"Well…my friends aren't exactly good guys, if you catch my drift. If she's looking for a fun night, I can arrange that. But if she's looking for a boyfriend, not so much."

"Honestly, I don't know what she's looking for."

"Since she's your best friend, you should ask her."

***

Rex and Zeke were sitting on the couch when I walked inside. Safari was sitting alone on the other couch, his eyes closed as he took a nap. The TV was on and a basketball game played.

"When are you moving out?" I tossed my purse on the table and entered the living room.

"Uh, hello to you too." Rex dogged me then took a drink of his beer.

"Hi," I said. "And when are you moving out?"

"Damn, Groovy Bowl just opened three days ago."

"And business was booming. So you should be able to get the hell out right about now." Safari and I needed our space. I could give Ryker a key, and he could come and go as he pleased, preferably naked.

"I don't know how much cash I have until the end of the month." He turned his gaze back to the TV in a failed attempt to ignore me.

"But you should have enough to make rent so you should start looking for a place—pronto."

"Damn, are you going to hound me to pay you back too?"

"No. You can keep that. I just want you out of my space." I walked back to the kitchen. "Hi, Zeke."

"Hey, Rae." He held up his beer in acknowledgment.

I poured a glass of wine then sat on the couch with Safari.

He opened his eyes and saw me then scooted closer until his chin rested on my thigh. After I started to pet him, he closed his eyes.

"Do you guys have any single friends?" I asked.

"Did you break up with Ryker?" Zeke blurted out the sentence so loud it sounded like a shout.

"Did you kick him to the curb?" Rex asked hopefully. "I knew you would see reason eventually. That guy is—"

"I'm asking for Kayden. But I'm glad to hear you guys finally accept Ryker..."

"Oh..." Rex deflated like a popped balloon.

Zeke drank his beer then stared at the floor. "I have a few, but I'm not sure if Kayden would like them."

"And none of my friends are good enough," Rex said.

"You don't have any doctor friends?" I asked Zeke. "The rich and good-looking type?"

"None that are young or good-looking," he said.

"Kayden needs to get laid?" Rex asked. "I can help her out with that. When we went out last month, she wore this tight black dress and damn, she looked so fuckable. Her legs went up to her neck."

"Ew." I was about to drink my wine but thought better of it. "Don't talk about my friend like that."

"What?" Rex asked innocently. "I'm just being honest. She cleans up good."

"Well," I said. "She cleans up well."

Rex had a blank look on his face. "What?"

I shook my head. "Never mind."

Zeke leaned forward with his arms resting on his knees. "Has she tried Tinder?"

"I don't think so," I said. "But I doubt she's looking for a hookup. I think she's more serious than that."

"There's eHarmony and stuff like that," Rex said. "But seriously, I could show her a good time."

I rolled my eyes. "Rex."

He rolled his eyes back at me. "I mean, I could show her a *well* time."

I smacked my hand to my forehead and dragged it across my face. He was hopeless.

Zeke smirked but didn't bother correcting him.

"So no?" I asked. "Neither one of you have any good guys to recommend?"

They both shook their heads in response.

"I guess I'll just go out with her and help her scoop up a guy." I hadn't been out with the girls in a while anyway. It would be nice to get dressed up and get out of the apartment, especially since my brother was permanently parked on the couch.

"Don't dress too nice," Zeke warned. "Otherwise, all the guys will go for you instead of her."

"Yeah, okay," I said with a laugh.

Zeke didn't change his expression.

"Well, I'm gonna get in the shower. You girls have fun tonight."

Rex stuck his tongue out at me. "Tell the other gremlins I said hello."

***

I met Kayden outside the bar. She wore a short black dress that showed off her killer legs, silver heels, and a silver clutch was tucked under her arm. Her hair was done in humongous curls, making her look like a beauty queen contestant. I looked her up and down when I reached her. "Damn, I think I might be bi."

She laughed before she hugged me. "Yeah right. With Ryker's package, you're straight to the bone."

"Very true."

She pulled away and looked at my pink dress. "You look so cute. I love that color on you."

"Thanks. So, are you ready to pick up a fine ass man to take home?"

She crossed her fingers. "Let's hope I get lucky."

"I invited Jess to come along but she said she's bitch-zilla because she started her period today."

Kayden cringed. "She did mankind a service by staying home."

"Word."

We entered the bar and pushed through the crowd to get our drinks. I noticed every guy in the room was staring at Kayden, so she would probably hook up with someone quick. I could duck out and go to Ryker's for some sweet action.

We got our drinks then walked to a free table in the center of the room. There were no chairs so we stood there in our five inch heels. We were both in pain, but according to girl code, you weren't allowed to complain no matter how excruciating it was. If you chose fashion over comfort, you were stuck with it.

"See anyone you like?" I glanced around the room and saw a few good-looking guys. But most of them were already making moves on different chicks.

Kayden glanced around the room casually. "Not particularly. But it's pretty early. The best ones come out late."

"True." More like, the bad ones.

Kayden sipped her drink and continued to glance around. "Thanks for coming out with me tonight. I know you already have a man so this may seem boring."

"Nah. It's always fun to hang with you. I just hope you take someone home."

"Me too…"

"So where did this need for a man come from?" She wasn't overly boy crazy, about the same as Jess and me. We were always looking for Mr. Right but it didn't control our lives.

She shrugged her petite shoulders, and when she moved, her diamond earrings sparkled under the dim lighting. "I just realized I haven't been out with anyone for a while. And if I don't go out to a bar, then how am I going to meet someone? It's not very often a guy my age walks into the library."

There was no worse place to meet someone. The only people who used public libraries were retired folks. Since Kayden wasn't a gold digger, that wasn't an option. "Well, there are definitely men your age here tonight."

Her head turned to the corner and she narrowed her eyes.

"See something you like?"

She continued to squint. "Doesn't that guy look like Ryker?"

I turned in her direction and narrowed my eyes on the booth in the corner. The guy Kayden was referring to was sitting on the right, and two other men took up the circular booth. Each guy had a woman under his arm. Ryker appeared to be alone.

He better be alone.

"Yeah, I think that's him."

"Did you tell him you were going out tonight?"

"No." Come to think of it, I hadn't spoken to him since my cab ride home. He usually asked me to do something the second I was free, but he obviously had other plans.

"You don't think he's with some skank, right?" She gave me a look of trepidation, like she hoped she was wrong.

The thought never crossed my mind. "No. I'm sure he's here alone." Ryker was difficult for me to read, but he would never do that to me. He wasn't a liar, and he wasn't disloyal either. "He's probably just with some friends."

"Yeah, you're probably right."

A tall brunette walked to their table and sat beside Ryker. She was beautiful, painfully so, and she rocked her heels like they were sandals. Ryker didn't touch her and barely looked at her, but I still didn't like the fact she was there.

Kayden turned her gaze back on me but she didn't say anything.

"Let's go say hi." I left the booth and knew she was behind me without looking. I wouldn't jump to any conclusions because Ryker wasn't doing anything wrong. If he wanted to go out for a drink with his friends, he had every right to do so. And just because his friends found hook-ups didn't mean he did too. That third woman might be friends with the other two and that was it. No need to panic.

I reached their booth and looked down at Ryker with Kayden beside me.

It took him a moment to realize I was there. When his eyes settled on me, he didn't seem as surprised as he should be. "Small world, huh?" He gave me his naturally charismatic smile like always.

And that told me everything was fine. If he'd been caught doing something he shouldn't, his reaction would have been a lot more skittish. Now I felt guilty for letting the thought even cross my mind.

Ryker would never do that to me, and I felt like a bitch for not implicitly trusting him to begin with. "I'd say so."

He turned to his friends. "That's Ryan and Leana." He turned to his other friend. "That's Jeremy and Wynona." Then he turned to the mystery woman sitting right beside him. "And Tisha. You guys, these are my friends Rae and Kayden."

Friends?

We were his friends?

I was his friend?

Kayden tensed beside me, just as offended as I was.

I kept my cool even though I was a volcano about to explode. His choice of words was a slap in the face. I probably wouldn't have cared if he got out of his seat and kissed me or something, but he continued to sit there like we hardly knew each other.

Like we weren't sleeping together.

After all the shit he gave me about telling Rex and Zeke about the two of us, he had the audacity to introduce me as a friend?

A friend?

Kayden grabbed my shoulder and gave me a gentle pull. His glass of scotch was on the table, and I had the urge to grab it and throw it in his face. She could read my mind as well as Jess, and she knew it was coming. Throwing alcohol in people's faces was somewhat my forte'.

I looked Ryker in the eye, pretty much flipping him the bird with my threatening gaze. "Have a good night. *Friend*." I turned on my heel and walked off with my shoulders back and my head held high. I didn't put up with bullshit, and that behavior was the definition of bullshit. If he chose to act like we weren't together, then fine. We weren't together.

"I can't believe that little prick." Kayden's voice picked up the second we were out of earshot. "He's such a dick."

"I know. I wanted to slap him."

"And throw that drink in his face. I saw you eyeing it."

If only I was a little closer.

"Rae."

I heard his voice come from behind me, but I didn't want to deal with him. I honestly wasn't expecting him to chase me at all. And I was hoping he wouldn't. "Keep going." I pulled Kayden with me and pretended not to hear him.

"Rae." He caught up to me and grabbed my other arm. "What was that?"

"Seriously?" Now that I was looking him in the face, I was even more pissed. Those beautiful green eyes no longer held any charm, and I was too angry to melt for his stern jaw and impressive shoulders. "I need to tell you something about me because you clearly don't know it already." I poked him hard in the chest and felt my finger ache from hitting the hard surface. "I'm not the kind of woman who waits around for some guy. I don't date men who aren't man enough to tell their friends I'm his. I don't play games, and I don't lie. You clearly don't fit the bill for me, Ryker. So I'm done with you." I turned away because I didn't want to look at him anymore. I just wanted to get away and tell Rex he was right. I never should have gotten involved with this playboy.

"Whoa, hold on." Ryker grabbed me by the wrist and yanked me into his chest. "What the hell are you so worked up about?"

"You introduced me as a friend. You didn't get off your ass to even hug me, and that cunt looked pretty comfortable as she practically sat in your lap. Ryker, if you can't handle a woman like me, that's fine. Because I'll find someone who can."

He grabbed both of my wrists and pinned them to my sides so I couldn't move. Kayden must have stepped away because this conversation was awkward to anyone who had ears. "First of all, what am I supposed to introduce you as?"

"Uh, your girlfriend?"

"I didn't think we were there yet."

Ouch. That was a slap in the face. "You're the one who wanted to date monogamously. If that doesn't make me your girlfriend, what does?"

"I thought we were just seeing each other."

"Then that disqualifies me as a friend, which was how you introduced me."

"I can't believe you're getting so worked up over this." He shook his head slightly with a tense jaw.

"You're the one who demanded I tell Rex and Zeke we were seeing each other."

"So I wouldn't have to sneak around behind their backs like some kind of pussy," he barked. "And before you explode, I told Ryan and Jeremy I was seeing you. So when I introduced you to them, they knew exactly who you were. The only reason why I didn't get up was because Tisha just sat down, and I didn't want to ask her to get up again. You're blowing this completely out of proportion right now."

I felt a little stupid, but I was also still pissed. "You would flip if I introduced you to someone as a friend and you know it."

"To an ex, sure. But to random people you'll never see again, no."

"And Tisha seemed interested in you."

"So what?" He continued to squeeze my wrists. "She asked if I wanted to go back to her apartment about twenty minutes ago. That's when I told everyone I was seeing you. Who cares if she wants my nuts when you're the only woman who gets to touch them." He pulled me closer into his chest, practically yanking me. "I'm sure they're watching right now, and it's pretty fucking clear I'm pussy-whipped. So will you calm the fuck down now?"

My chest ached with every deep breath I took, and I couldn't make the humiliation burning in my cheeks stop. But I was still angry, upset all of this happened in the first place. If he'd just addressed me more personally, I wouldn't have stormed off. So, it was still his fault in my eyes. "Good night, Ryker." I just wanted to go home and be alone. I had some thinking to do. I pulled out of his grasp and turned on my heel.

"That's it?" he asked incredulously. "End of story?"

I turned back around. "End of relationship—or whatever the hell this is." My rage was doing all the talking, and I said things I didn't mean. I didn't want to lose Ryker. In fact, I wanted him more. I wanted him to call me his girlfriend and jump out of that booth to kiss me where everyone could see.

Ryker grabbed me again, and this time, he pulled me outside to the cool air. The music thudded from inside the building, the bass bouncing against the walls. A short line was outside as people waited to get in. He pulled me to the sidewalk and kept his hold on my elbow. "This isn't over."

"Yes. It. Is."

"Why?" he demanded. "Over that stupid little misunderstanding?"

I threw his arm down so he wouldn't touch me again. "No! I've never been this jealous in my life. I've never wanted someone so much before. And I'm just realizing how much I've fallen, how deep in the hole I'm getting. And if you won't even call me your girlfriend...then I'm setting myself up for failure. If I could be so easily hurt by that introduction, then that tells me you already mean more to me than you should. I thought I could guard my heart and play it cool, but I guess I can't. That's why I'm ending this." I stepped back so I would be out of reach if he tried to grab me again.

He stared at me, vapor rising out of his nose with every breath he took. He wore a long-sleeved, gray t-shirt and dark jeans, and despite the cold, he looked so warm. His eyes were full of fire, like he was angry at me for everything I just said.

I crossed my arms over my chest because I was cold. My nipples were poking through the fabric. Tonight was supposed to be carefree and fun, but it ended up being a disaster instead. I was doomed to repeat my mistakes and fall for guys who always broke my heart. Why couldn't I change the cycle? Why couldn't I pull my head out of my ass and think clearly for once?

"Rae, this is new to me. And I'm scared too."

My eyes found his and saw the sincerity.

He stepped closer to me, but I didn't back up. "I know we have our problems, and we need to work on them. But I don't want to break up. I don't want to stop seeing you, stop kissing you, and stop making love to you."

It was one of the few times he said something sweet, and I felt my heart race as it fluttered.

"I'll be your boyfriend if that's what you want."

"I want you to want it too…"

"I want to be with you. That's all I know. If you want me to introduce you as my girlfriend, then I will. If you want me to introduce you as the Queen of Seattle, I'll do that too. Whatever you want."

Finally, my lips formed a smile.

He wrapped his arms around my waist and pulled me close. "Did I fix it?"

I nodded. "I think you did."

"Want to go back in there, and I'll introduce you the proper way?"

I chuckled because I thought he was joking. "Unnecessary."

"Because I will, Rae. Whatever you want."

I pressed my face against his chest and inhaled his masculine scent. "It's really okay."

He rested his chin on my head and kept his arms tight around me. "Sweetheart, you're freezing. How about we go back to my place?"

"Even if I weren't freezing, I'd want to do that."

He kissed my temple then walked me down the sidewalk to his car. "Good. Me too."

***

"You have some making up to do." Ryker stripped off his clothes then lay on the bed, his back against the headboard and his long dick resting against his hard stomach. He interlocked his fingers behind his head and stared me down, that smoldering look on his face.

"Me?" I placed both of my hands on my hips and cocked my head. My attitude was forced. I wasn't the least bit annoyed. In fact, anytime I saw him buck naked, I was aroused. My thighs wanted to squeeze together in longing, and my breathing had already changed. My mouth was dry and desperate to wrap around his shaft, forming a suction so tight he'd come immediately. "I remember tonight quite differently."

"I guess we have a difference of opinion." He patted the mattress beside him. "Now get over here."

I didn't want to participate in our usual bickering. The fact that he showed me a new level of commitment settled my unease. My jealousy left my body quicker than I could understand, and the ache in my chest was one of the most painful experiences I'd ever felt. Just when I thought things were casual, I realized they were far more serious than that—at least in my heart.

I stripped away my clothes but took my time, giving him a mini strip show. I dropped the articles of clothing until I got to the bright pink thong around my hips. I played with the lace for nearly a minute, drawing it out as long as possible.

Ryker's eyes were glued to my panties, and his fingers immediately wrapped around his shaft and gently massaged it. "Give it to me, sweetheart."

I pulled the thong off then kicked it away. I stood stark naked in just my black heels. On a whim, I decided not to take them off. I crawled across the bed and straddled his hips, my heels digging into the sheets on either side of him.

His hands grazed over my thighs then rested on my hips. He immediately pointed his head at my entrance and shoved himself inside, not bothering to take his time like he usually did. His powerful chest rose and fell with heavy breaths, and his shoulders were tense with desperation. He stared at my tits as they hung right in front of his face. When he slowly slid inside me, he released a quiet moan of satisfaction. "Why would I want anyone else when I have this?" He moved completely inside me until his entire shaft was sheathed. He rolled his head back slightly against the headboard and closed his eyes, enjoying the sensation of our bodies combined together.

I heard what he said but I couldn't process his meaning. Feeling him inside me, so thick and so long, brought a shadow over my eyes so I couldn't even think. It was a heavy fog, a realm of confusion and pleasure. I'd never been with a man who had such an impressive package. It was worth all the bickering, arguing, and uncertainty.

His hands migrated to my tits and he squeezed them in his large hands. "Fuck me, sweetheart."

I gripped his shoulders and used their sturdiness as an anchor to take him over and over. I started off slow and intended to stay that way, but heat scorched through me and fueled me forward. I bounced on his dick hard and fast, working up a sweat within minutes.

He played with my nipples before he moved his hands to my ass. He squeezed my cheeks hard then guided me up and down his length, yanking me forcefully down his cock. The distinct sound of our friction played on our ears, and I knew I was soaking wet without even checking. "You look damn perfect when you ride my cock like that."

I gripped the rails of his headboard and leaned forward, my tits in his face.

He immediately lathered my flesh with kisses, pulling my nipples into his mouth and sucking them. "You make me want to come so hard."

"Not just yet." Ryker had never left me hanging before and he better not now.

He pressed his face into my neck and gave a slight chuckle. "My woman takes what she wants...fucking hot." He kissed my neck and the shell of my ear as he pressed his fingers to my clit and rubbed it aggressively, trying to get me off so he could fill my pussy with every ounce of his cum.

Like always, I felt the sensation burn deep inside my belly before it rushed out everywhere else. Like a scorching fire that scorched me to the bone, I turned into an inferno of heat. I tightened around his dick and locked eyes with him as my body crumbled in ecstasy. "God, yes…" My nails dug into his shoulders and my hips immediately bucked.

He pulled me completely down his length just as he released inside me, giving me everything he had. His cock twitched inside me, and the weight of his seed filled my pussy with substance. He kissed me, sweat from his upper lip mixing with mine. "Call me Ryker."

***

Jenny held up the phone. "It's your girl, Kayden."

I knew exactly what she was calling about. "Thanks. I'll take it over here."

Jenny put the phone back on the hook then returned to her side of the lab, her white lab coat hanging all the way down to her knees.

I grabbed the phone and hit Line 1. "Hey."

"What happened last night?" She didn't bother saying hi or anything else. She wanted the dirt, and I didn't blame her after seeing the fight Ryker and I had at the bar. "I saw the two of you going at it like alley cats."

Strange comparison, but whatever. "It's a long story…" I glanced at Jenny across the lab to see if she could hear me. "So I was pissed at—" I couldn't say his name because Jenny would figure out I was dating the boss. That was delicate information I couldn't allow to slip into the ether. When Ryker and I were more serious, possibly living together, then I would come clean about it. "Tom because he didn't even acknowledge me to his friends—"

"Tom?"

"Just go with it."

"Uh, alright. But why?"

"Just because." I moved past it. "So we argued outside and—"

"Oh!" The realization dawned on her. "Because he's your boss. Gotcha."

She was a little slow sometimes. "Exactly. Anyway, we argued outside for a while and he explained that he already told them he was dating me, so introducing me by my name was enough. But we argued a little while longer and had great make up sex later."

"Girl, when he introduced you as his friend, I almost went postal."

I did go postal. "I was ticked too."

"And that skank sitting next to him wanted to jump his bones. I could totally tell."

Every woman wanted to jump his bones. I had to get used to it. "I know. But he said I was his girlfriend so everything is okay."

"Still pissed me off. No one treats my friend like that."

I smiled at her loyalty. "I know you've got my back."

"Since you guys worked everything out, I guess I'll let it go. But I was prepared to knock his teeth out."

"I got brass knuckles in my purse so I had it covered. But thanks." That wasn't a joke. I really did have a pair for protection. "Sorry I ruined your night. Did you meet anyone?"

"No," she said with a sigh. "I left shortly after you guys did. But maybe next time."

"Sorry. We can go out again. Maybe Jess can come next time."

"So she can steal all the guys?" she asked with a laugh. "No, thanks."

"Whatever, Kayden. You're all that and a bag of chips. Don't play dumb."

"I'm not playing dumb," she argued. "I just know guys like her dark hair and smoky eyes. Sometimes I find myself checking her out."

I chuckled. "Me too. She has the perfect body."

"And the prettiest face."

I pictured Rex and Zeke listening to this conversation. Their jaws would be on the floor and their eyes would pop out of their heads. "Could you imagine if the guys overheard us?"

"Oh god. They would pass out."

"They would probably hand us whipped cream and Jell-O." Maybe not Rex, but Zeke definitely would. "By the way, I asked the guys if they had any friends to set you up with but they said no. Then Rex said he would love to show you a good time." I rolled my eyes. "He's such a sleazy pervert."

"Wait. What? Rex likes me?" Her voice suddenly came out high-pitched and squeaky.

"I wouldn't say he likes you. He just said he wouldn't mind giving you a nice hook-up if that's what you're looking for. So be prepared next time you see him. He might be a bit of a sleazebag."

Kayden was dead silent. Her breathing couldn't even be heard over the line.

"Kay?"

"Yeah, I'm here." Now her voice was back to normal but still rushed. "I need to get back to work. I'll talk to you later."

"Uh, okay." It was an abrupt end to our conversation, but I needed to get back to work too. The gel electrophoresis couldn't run itself. "Talk to you later."

"Bye." Click.

Before I had a chance to dwell on the conversation, Jenny called me over. "Rae, come take a look at this."

The prospect of a scientific discovery masked all other thoughts, and I didn't think about our conversation any longer. "Coming, Jen."

Ray of Hope

Chapter Four

Rex

Even on a Thursday, Groovy Bowl was hopping.

Most of the lanes were being used, families were in the pizza parlor, and even the bar had a few regulars. I barely had enough workers to man the place, so I immediately began hiring more help.

My original plan when I bought the place was just to do the books then go home before noon every day, but now that the place had been remodeled, I liked the atmosphere. It was a cool place to hang out, and the laid back feel made everyone forget their problems. The place even smelled good. I didn't notice how bad it stank until everything had been swapped out.

Rae was right. The place did smell like cat piss.

I had interviews with a few college kids that wanted part time work, and by the time that was finished, it was almost four in the afternoon. Time flew by, and it didn't feel like a miserable day at work like it used to.

It was actually fun.

When I broke down the register to put cash into the safe, I was surprised we even had cash to stow away. Normally, there was just a few one dollar bills and some paper clips. I waded the cash into a rubber band then tucked it into my pocket. At this rate, I would be able to pay back Rae and Zeke in no time.

"Hey, Rex."

I looked over the counter and came face-to-face with Kayden. Her blonde hair was pulled in a high ponytail, showing off the pretty features of her face. She had dark makeup around her eyes, and golden hoops hung from her lobes. All the guys in the place immediately turned her way once they noticed her, seeing her perfection just as slowly as I did. "Hey. What brings you here?"

"I just got off work and wanted to see how the place was doing. It looks great."

"Thanks. Rae and Zeke did a great job."

"As did you." She gave me a soft look, almost like she was proud of me.

I shrugged. "I really can't take any credit. Without them, this place would have gone under and I would have lived with Rae for the rest of my life." Then shot myself in the head because she drove me insane.

"You're always so humble."

I wasn't even sure what that word meant. "How did the other night go? Pick up some fine piece of ass?"

"No. Rae and Ryker got into a big fight so I just went home."

Joy exploded inside me like a firework. "They broke up?"

"No. They made up later."

That happiness disappeared instantly. "Why was he there?"

"He was hanging out with some friends. He introduced Rae as a friend and she got upset."

"As she should." I would be on my sister's side no matter what, even if she was dead wrong. I knew Ryker was bad news, and it was only a matter of time before Rae came home in tears. I wanted to be wrong but I knew I wouldn't be so lucky.

"But they cleared it up. Then I went home solo."

"I'm surprised all the guys in the bar didn't swoop down on you."

She quickly broke eye contact and smiled. "There are beautiful women in every bar in Seattle. I don't stand out."

"Yeah, okay," I said with a snort. I remembered the way she looked in that tiny black dress. I wanted it to rise up a few more inches so I could see what her panties looked like. She got me harder than steel the instant I looked at her—and that was the highest level of hottest. All this talk about her appearance was giving me an instant boner right behind the counter. I needed to change the subject. Otherwise, I would need to go in my office and rub one out so all other functions would continue like normal.

"So, how's it going down here?"

"Good. I hired more people so things will go smoothly. I'm excited that I can actually pay Rae and Zeke back. That was my biggest worry."

"We all knew this would be a success. Your stress was for nothing." She continued to stand at the counter and didn't seem intent on leaving. And our conversation was normal, not awkward and weird like it usually was.

Maybe the curse had been lifted. "I'm getting off right now." I realized how I phrased it and my hard on came back. "I mean, I'm clocking out. You wanna get some food? I'm starving because I skipped lunch today."

"That sounds like a great idea. Where do you want to go?"

"How about Mega Shake?" I could eat a burger and fries every single day.

"That sounds fabulous."

***

Kayden devoured her food like I'd never seen before. She usually picked at her food like some kind of rabbit, but now she ate like a real person. Her actions reminded me of Rae, and it didn't surprise me they were best friends.

"What do you think of Ryker?" Were Rae's friends just as smitten over him? Or did they see him as trouble too?

"What do you mean?" She sipped her milkshake, her lips sucking on the straw and making me imagine her sucking something else.

My mind was seriously in the gutter today. "Do you think he's good for her? Or is he just going to break her heart?"

"He'll probably break her heart." She said it simply and without any emotion. "But that's how all relationships end. None of them end happily. I don't think Ryker is as bad of a guy as you make him seem. Honestly, he's not any different than you or Zeke."

That was offensive. "Zeke and I are totally different."

She narrowed her eyes in the form of a challenge.

"Okay, we're oddly similar. But I would never date Ryker's sister no matter how hot she was."

She gave me the same look again.

"I really wouldn't." I understood boundaries and I didn't cross them. If there was anything I respected, it was family. I wish Ryker felt the same.

"You really shouldn't waste your time worrying about the two of them. Rae asked you to butt out, and it sounds like you aren't doing that."

I couldn't deny the accusation. "The only reason why I'm asking is because you said they had a fight."

"All couples fight, Rex. Doesn't mean anything."

I just wished it was the last fight they had—and they'd finally called it quits. I knew Rae and Zeke would never have a chance together, but that didn't mean there wasn't someone better out there for Rae. I always pictured her settling down with a good-looking nerd. They'd have three kids, and I'd live in the guest house because I never got my shit together. "You're right. I shouldn't think about it."

She sucked on her milkshake again, her cheeks hollowing.

I wished those lips would suck me off right now. "So..."

She pulled her lips away for some air. "What?"

"Huh?"

Her eyes narrowed. "You just said so."

"I did?"

"Yeah..."

I couldn't even think straight. "How's the library?" My cock was pressed against the zipper in my jeans, and it was extremely uncomfortable. I would adjust it in front of almost anyone, but I didn't want

Kayden to know I wanted to fuck her right on the table and lick her milkshake off her tits.

"It's good. Really quiet."

"Must be nice." I listened to bowling balls crash against pins all day.

"It is. Allows me to get a lot of reading done."

"That's cool. Getting paid to read." This wasn't working either. Every time I pictured her in the library, she wore a black skirt with reading glasses on the bridge of her nose. She was stern but naughty, and she took me into the sea of books so we could fuck against a bookshelf.

"I love it. I can see myself working there for the rest of my life. But the pay sucks."

"Money is just money."

"Yeah, but my tiny little apartment won't be suitable forever."

"When you get married, the second income will be enough." I was jealous of her non-existent husband. He'd get to fuck her every night while I'd just have my hand.

"Yeah...maybe."

I sipped my milkshake just so I had something to do while I tried to think about something other than my dick between her tits. I was a horn dog, but I'd never been this bad before. I could usually control my thoughts when I was around a beautiful woman, but right now, I was a slave to my sexual instincts.

"There's something I wanted to ask you...and it might be a little weird."

That finally got me to focus. "Okay."

"I'm a little embarrassed to talk about it because...well, it's embarrassing."

"You can tell me anything, and I won't make fun of you." I was the most embarrassing person on the planet. I bought a bowling alley, and I lived with my younger sister. I was almost thirty years old, and I hadn't accomplished anything with my life. I couldn't laugh at anyone because I was the one people should be laughing at.

"Well...I'm not very experienced." She stared at me like that simple sentence explained everything she was trying to say. She searched my gaze for a reaction, looking for something specific.

"I don't understand what you mean. Inexperienced? As in, you want to spice up your resume?"

"No, not my resume." She held back a chuckle and her cheeks flushed red. "I mean, I'm not sexually experienced."

I stared at her blankly, picturing her naked on my bed. Her hands would run up my chest until they stopped at my shoulders. Then she'd cry out when I thrust myself inside her. Anytime a beautiful woman even mentioned the word sex, I pictured myself fucking her. It was a guy thing so I shouldn't be judged for it. "Oh..." That was all I could get myself to say. Now my cock was throbbing.

"I don't know what I'm doing. I don't have any confidence. Honestly, I'm clueless."

"You're dead wrong, Kayden. You're the sexiest woman in every room you walk into. You don't need to have any moves because you're hot. All you have to do is lie there, and you'll get a perfect score." I'd do all the work if she were on my bed.

Her cheeks continued to burn the same color. "That's nice of you to say but…I need a lot of help."

"Help?" What did that mean?

"This is where the awkward part comes in."

I held my breath.

"You've been around the block a few times and know exactly what guys want. I would love it if you taught me a few things…"

This was too good to be true. I opened my mouth to speak but nothing came out. My voice had disappeared due to the shock. I covered my mouth and cleared my throat before I finally got something out. "When you say teach you a few things…what does that mean exactly?"

"Teaching me how to talk to guys. Teaching me how to make a pass at someone I like…"

So boring stuff that she didn't even need help with. My excitement vanished.

"How to kiss a guy. How to give a good blow job…"

What the fuck did she just say?

"How to be good in bed…stuff like that."

Was she serious? Did I just win the fucking lottery again? "You want me to teach you how to give good head?" Was she messing with me right now? Was this just a big joke? If it was, I didn't even care for that I fell for it.

"Yeah…if that's something you'd want to do. If not, I totally understand. We're friends and things could get weird. I just wanted to do this with someone I'm comfortable with, someone who knows what they're doing. It's really not a big deal if you say no—"

"Say no?" I asked with a laugh. "My answer is yes. A million times over—yes." I leaned forward and felt my hands shake with excitement. My cock was desperate for release and was going to break through the zipper at any moment. "I'll gladly teach you anything you could possibly want to know—from the basics to the Olympics."

"I'm glad I didn't make things awkward between us."

"Hell no. You just made my day."

"Yeah?"

"Absolutely. You're one of the hottest girls I've ever seen. Watching you suck that milkshake was torture."

"Really? I—"

"When can we start?"

She chuckled, her cheeks finally returning to their normal color. "I don't know. I thought—"

"How about now? Let's go to your place."

"Uh, okay. But maybe we should lay down some ground rules."

I hated rules.

"I think we should keep this between us. That includes not mentioning this to Zeke."

I told Zeke everything. But I understood her request. He would probably tell Rae and Jess, and that would be a weird conversation to have. If I was giving her shit about Ryker, she could easily give me shit about this. "That's fine. What else?"

"That's it."

I jumped out of the chair so fast I knocked it over. "Then let's get going."

"Right now?" she asked incredulously.

"What? You have plans?"

"No, but I—"

"Then let's get started."

***

She had a one-bedroom apartment that was half the size as Rae's place. If I had to share this space with my sister, I really would kill myself. I'd never been there before, and I took a moment to notice the way she decorated it. All the furniture was white, and vases of fresh flowers were everywhere. It was definitely a woman's haven.

"Alright." I rubbed my hands together greedily before I sat on the couch. "Let's get started."

She left her purse by the door and hung up her coat before she joined me. A few minutes ago, she seemed calm, but now she was nervous. Her hands shook, and she couldn't look me in the eye. She pulled her limbs closer to her body and tried to appear as small as possible.

I grabbed her hand and held it on my thigh. The second I touched her, I felt the longing deep in my bones. Her fingers were slender and warm. They would feel amazing all over my body, particularly wrapped around my cock. "Don't be nervous."

"Can't help it."

I grabbed her chin and forced her gaze directly on me. Her eyes were bright blue and made of crystal. I never noticed them before, how clear they were. Her skin was soft under my touch. Her scent washed over me, smelling like summer and strawberries. "So where should we start?" I wanted to go straight into the bedroom and take all my clothes off, but that was jumping the gun.

"I don't know. I guess I don't know how to talk to a guy."

"I don't understand what you mean. You really don't need to do anything. They'll come to you."

A small smile formed on her lips. "I appreciate the compliment, but guys almost never hit on me."

"Bullshit."

"I'm serious."

"I'll never believe that no matter how many times you say it."

"You think I'm lying?"

"No. But I think you're confused." If I didn't know Kayden as my sister's friend, I would have hit on her a long time ago. But she was off limits so I kept my distance. Now that she asked for a teacher, I didn't feel any guilt for what I was about to do. I helped her, and I got something in the process.

"I'm not confused."

"Alright. Let's start from the beginning. Let's pretend I'm a guy you're interested in. You walk over to me and then say what?" I let go of her hand. "Where do you start?"

She shrugged. "I don't know…"

"Come on. You're face-to-face with a stranger and you say nothing?"

"Uh…hi."

Her lack of confidence shocked me since she was ridiculously gorgeous. She had a perfect face and a perfect body. A woman like her didn't need to chase anyone down. They came to her. I didn't want to be too hard on her because she was self-conscious, so I gave her a gentle nudge. "Men respond to confidence. We hate it when women are conceited. That's just annoying. But confidence is sexy as hell."

"How do I act confident?"

"When you talk to me, act like I'm the one who could get a great opportunity."

"Okay…how?"

"Just say hello and introduce yourself."

"Okay." She cleared her throat. "Hi. I'm Kayden."

"Perfect." I gave her a thumbs up. "I'm Rex. Nice to meet you."

She stared at me blankly because she didn't know what else to do.

"Now you can do one of two things. You can either make a comment about the situation or my preference or just come out and tell him you think he's hot."

"What?" she asked incredulously. "Desperate, much?"

"It's not desperate. It's confident." Big difference. "Now tell me you think I'm cute or something."

She tucked a loose strand behind her ear. "I think—"

"Don't fidget. I can tell you're nervous. Don't let him know you're nervous."

"My god, I didn't know hitting on someone was so much work."

"Well, be grateful you're a woman."

She cleared her throat. "I think you're cute." She stared me in the eye as she said it and she didn't fidget.

"Great," I said. "If you're really into the guy, tell him you think he's sexy."

She cringed. "That's just weird."

"No, it's not."

"No one says that. Sexy? I think cute is more appropriate."

"But cute could describe a puppy or a kitten. Men are like women. We want to feel attractive too."

I met a few women who outright told me I was a sexy stud, and that really got me hard. "I'm telling you, he'd love it."

"I don't know…"

"Now tell me you think I'm sexy."

She straightened her shoulders and didn't fidget. "I think you're sexy."

I gave her a thumbs up again. "Perfect."

"Now what?"

"If he's not a dick, he'll say thank you. And then he'll ask you out or say he has a girlfriend."

"What if he doesn't ask me out?"

"Then you ask him out."

"Again, that feels desperate."

I held up my finger and shook it. "No. Confident."

"I don't know…"

"Trust me on this. You asked for my help for a reason, right?"

She sighed before she nodded.

"Then you'll have yourself a date. Bam."

"Hope so. But I don't know what to do on a date."

How did she not know how to do anything? She wasn't an alien, as far as I could tell. "Just be yourself."

"Easier said than done."

"You know what I think?"

"Hmm?"

"I don't think having 'moves' is a good way to go. Be yourself, and if they don't like you for who you are, then it's better that it doesn't work out. Don't give someone a good impression if it's not who you are. You want someone to want you exactly as you are. That's the only way you'll be happy."

Her eyes softened. "That's really wise…and sweet."

"What can I say? I'm a guru. So…let's get to the good stuff." I leaned closer to her and eyed her lips. "What do you want to work on?"

Her eyes glanced at my mouth before she looked at me head on. "I don't know how to be sexy all around. I'm pretty clueless."

"What are you talking about? You're being sexy right now."

"How?"

"Because you're stunning. Your hair is all pretty, your eyes are pretty, your skin is pretty...it's all good, Kay."

She cracked a smile. "But I don't know how to *be* sexy. I could sit here all day, but I'm not actually doing anything."

Now I understood what she meant. "Gotcha."

"When I kiss a guy...I don't know where to put my hands. I don't know how much tongue I should give. I don't know what a man wants when he kisses a woman. I feel awkward most of the time."

"Well, I can help you with that." I scooted closer to her on the couch until our faces were almost touching. My arm moved over the back of the couch and my hand rested on her opposite shoulder. I should've felt weird for coming on to my friend, but I didn't feel weird at all. I studied her pink lips, noting how plump and smooth they were. When I imagined kissing her, the taste of bubblegum filled my mouth.

Her eyes moved to my lips, and her chest stopped rising because she wasn't breathing. "Rex, how do you like a woman to kiss you?" Her words escaped as a sexy whisper and trickled down my spine.

I was already hard, but now my cock was made of steel.

My hand moved up her shoulder until it reached the back of her neck. I lightly felt the smooth strands as they were pulled back into her ponytail. The pulse in her neck thudded against my fingertips. "I like a slow kiss. Harder and faster isn't necessarily better. I like to feel her lips and let her feel mine. And I love it when her tongue slips into my mouth once in a while, gently."

Her lips were slightly parted and she began to breathe hard. Her cheeks were flushed, but not from embarrassment. "How do you like to be touched?"

"Everywhere. Anywhere."

Her hand snaked to my thigh where she gave it a gentle squeeze.

She was so close to my cock.

She closed her eyes and leaned in, her lips pressing against mine with a sexy softness. Her lips felt full like I imagined, and instead of giving me an awkward kiss like I expected, she felt my upper lip with hers. She sucked on it gently before she pulled the bottom one into her mouth.

I was too stunned to do anything.

She squeezed my thigh then deepened the kiss, not increasing her pace but intensifying her touch. She breathed into my mouth gently before continuing, her chest pressed into mine. Her hand slowly slid up my thigh and across my stomach. When she reached my chest, she rested her hand over my heart, feeling it beat.

Damn.

She hooked one arm around my neck and pulled her body closer. Her lips cherished mine with sexy desperation, and she purposely pressed the swell of her tits right against me. She sucked my bottom lip again before she breathed into my mouth.

Oh my fucking god.

Her hands continued to move across my body, feeling the lines of muscle in my chest and my arms. When her hand moved to my cheek, she cupped it and gave me a small amount of her tongue.

Yes.

She crawled farther into my lap and straddled my hips. My neck went to the back of the couch and my mouth was tilted toward hers. She dug both of her hands into my hair and kissed me harder, wanting more of my mouth.

It was the best kiss I'd ever had.

She rocked her hips gently, sliding her bottom across the definition of my cock.

And she thought she didn't know how to be sexy?

My hands recovered from the amazing things her mouth was doing to me, and they moved across her body. I felt the steep curve in her back, noting just how prominent it was. I was a sucker for that curve, and hers was off the hook.

Her kiss was making me a little crazy so my hands migrated to her ass where I squeezed both cheeks through her jeans. Perky, firm, and perfect. My fingers dug into the fabric, and I wished I could feel her naked skin.

My hands moved to her hips and slender waist. I could feel the small muscles of her core working to rock into me and kiss me at the same time. I could feel her strength as well as her feminine curves.

She was perfect.

She followed my directions perfectly and executed my orders like a commander. She took control with sexy confidence and owned that kiss like she did it for a living. I should've ended the embrace so we could move on to something else, but I didn't have the strength to stop. I wanted to keep kissing her forever.

And never stop.

***

When it was dark inside her apartment, I knew it was late. We got to her place around five and since my stomach was growling, I knew it was at least ten in the evening. Our kiss lasted for hours, and I didn't get tired of it.

I haven't done that since eighth grade.

Kayden finally ended the kiss and pulled away, but her face was still close to mine. Her ponytail had come undone at some point, and her hair formed a curtain around me. Her lips were swollen and red from the make out session we just had, but she didn't seem to regret it. "Feedback?"

I stared at her blankly because I didn't have a damn thing to say.

She pulled farther away and shifted her hair over one shoulder, keeping it out of my face.

"That was…yeah."

"Yeah?"

"You nailed it, baby." I grabbed her hips and pulled her back into me, wanting to take her in the bedroom and fuck her senseless. "But practice makes perfect, right?" I wanted to lift her shirt and suck her nipples until they were raw.

"True."

"So, let's pick this up tomorrow after work." Who knew being a teacher would be so fulfilling?

"Okay."

I rolled her off me before I stood up. My cock was aching for release. Having a boner for four hours really pissed him off. I needed to shoot my cannon before I exploded. "I'll see you tomorrow. Should we meet here?"

"Yeah, sounds good." She walked me to the door, a slight smile on her lips.

I pretended not to notice. "Well, good night." Now that I'd kissed her for four hours, I didn't know how to say goodbye. Did I just wave like I usually did? Was I supposed to kiss her? Or was the physical affection only during lessons?

"Good night." She stayed by the door and didn't move to embrace me.

That answered my question. "Rest those lips. We have a lot of ground to cover."

***

I called Zeke when I got home.

"What's up?" He sighed into the phone like he was tired.

"What? You have a woman over there?"

"No. I'm in bed reading."

"Wow. Really living it up, huh?"

"It's ten thirty, dude. I have work in the morning."

"Still lame."

"Did you call for a reason?"

"Yeah…" I wanted to tell him what happened with Kayden but we agreed not to say anything. But I wanted to launch into details about those kisses we shared and how long it went on for. And I wanted to know if what I was doing was a really stupid idea or a great one. I got to fool around with a beautiful woman with no strings attached. There was no fear of her wanting more because she was just using me—and I was using her.

"Then what's up?"

"I just…never mind." Maybe when Kayden and I finished our project, I could tell him what happened. By then, everything would be in the past so it wouldn't matter. "I'll let you go."

"Are you sure there's nothing you want to talk about?"

"Yeah…I'll talk to you later." I hung up before he could ask me anything else.

Chapter Five

Rex

The clock couldn't go fast enough.

I loved Groovy Bowl and the transformation it just underwent. But all I really wanted to do was get off work and make out with Kayden—and whatever else she wanted to work on. She was so goddamn sexy that my cock wanted to bury itself inside her and never come out. I wanted to kiss every inch of her and never stop.

The situation was only temporary, and once she was comfortable with everything I taught her, she would be on her way to finding Mr. Right. But that didn't mean I couldn't enjoy every second of this. I was immensely attracted to her, and the fact she was off limits just made her irresistible.

When I was finally able to leave, I practically ran to her apartment. I would have taken an Uber but walking was actually quicker. I stopped myself from running even though my legs wanted to take off at full speed.

I finally reached her apartment and knocked louder than I meant to. The door shook under the force, and I realized I needed to chill out a bit.

She opened the door, looking just as beautiful as she did yesterday. "Hey, teach."

"Hey, student." When I walked inside, I had to stop myself from grabbing her and kissing her. We were doing these lessons for her benefit, not mine. I just got to enjoy the things she preferred to do. So I kept my hands to myself. "What lesson are we working on today?"

"I'm not sure. What do you recommend?" She wore black leggings with a long dress on top. It had long sleeves and covered most of her body from view, so I hoped whatever she had in mind involved taking her clothes off.

If she put the ball in my court, I knew exactly what I wanted to do. "You mentioned something about a blow job…" Act cool. Act cool.

"Yeah, I do need to work on that."

This was too good to be true. "Well…I'm at your service."

"Okay. Let's get started."

My jaw almost dropped. She was going to get on her knees and suck me off for practice? Seriously? "Uh…I'm probably going to regret saying this, but I need to say it anyway."

She was already at the couch.

"Maybe you should wait until you're in a relationship and tell the guy all of this. Trust me, he's not going to mind teaching you."

"Are you saying you don't want to do this?"

"Not. At. All." I wanted to do this more than anything else in my life. "I just…I don't really see what you get out of this." Despite my chivalrous attempt, my legs were already carrying me to the couch.

"I want to learn, and I want you to be the one who teaches me." She looked at me with those beautiful blue eyes. With the brightness of the stars, they hypnotized me. She wasn't begging, but just her asking me seemed like a plea. She could do this with any other guy but she wanted me. "Why?"

"Like I said, I know you know what you're doing."

"So do a lot of guys."

"Yeah, but we're good friends. I trust you."

I continued trying to be a gentleman, but I was losing the battle. "If you just see me as a friend, what do you get out of this?" I was immensely attracted to her so I got a lot out of this. If any beautiful woman asked me to make out with her, I'd do it in a heartbeat. But women were different about that sort of thing.

"I think you're sexy, Rex." She slowly walked toward me until her chest was pressed to mine. Her face hovered inches away, and her lips were kissable just as they were yesterday. Her hands snaked up my arms and gripped my biceps.

I took a deep breath as the pleasure radiated all over my body. Kayden thought I was sexy, and hearing her compliment me like that was such a turn on. I wanted my dick in her mouth—every inch.

"Teach me." She cupped my face and gave me a slow kiss.

I was a goner. Her whispers were always sexy, and those lips were fuckable. "It'd be my pleasure." My hands gripped her hips, and I kissed her harder, letting my attraction take the reins. I held her close to me, my lips devouring her with desperation. Every time I thought about my dick in her mouth, I almost came.

I guided her in front of the couch before I reluctantly pulled my lips away. "Lesson number one: a man never wants to ask for a blow job. You need to give it to him spontaneously. That's when we enjoy it the most."

"Yes, sir."

Fuck. Did she just call me sir? "Lesson number two: you need to take the lead the entire time. All confidence and all power. Undo my jeans and pull them off, my boxers too. Do it slowly, draw it out."

Her hands went to my jeans, and she unbuttoned them.

My spine shivered.

She got them loose and down my legs until they were around my ankles.

I loomed over her, feeling like a king. "Anytime you can get on your knees, you should."

She took my advice and lowered herself to the ground. Then she grabbed the brim of my boxers and slowly pulled them down.

I couldn't believe this was really happening.

She pulled them down my hips until my cock popped out. Long and hard, it was over the moon to see her face. He wanted to go deep and far down her throat until every inch was sheathed in that warm mouth.

She stared at my cock, her lips parted and her breathing became deep and loud. She moistened her lips with her tongue as she continued to look at every inch of my package. Then she leaned in and pressed a kiss to the center of my shaft, right over the large vein.

She was a natural.

She pulled my boxers down the rest of the way then gripped my thighs for balance. She looked up at me for direction, the desire heavy in her eyes like it was in mine.

The biggest turn on with a blow job was when a woman really wanted to do it. If it was out of obligation or duty, it wasn't nearly as sexy. And the look in her eyes told me she wanted my big fat cock in her mouth yesterday.

"Suck my balls." I grabbed the back of her neck and guided her mouth to my sack. "Take each one into your mouth and run your tongue across it."

Her lips brushed against my sack before she did as I commanded. She brought the sensitive skin into her mouth and sucked and licked like a pro. She used all of her saliva to lubricate the skin as she lathered me with kisses.

I could watch her all day. "Use your hand to jerk me."

She wrapped her hand against my shaft and slowly moved up and down, her tongue still working my balls.

This was the best day of my life. "You're doing great, baby." I grabbed a handful of hair and held it away from her face so there wasn't anything to interrupt her. I wanted her to go to town on my nuts and never stop.

She licked my balls like it was anything but a chore. She seemed to be into it, enjoying the feeling of my balls in her mouth as much as I did. She pleased me but teased me at the same time, building up to the best part—my cock in her mouth.

"Don't tease him for too long." I grabbed the base of my cock and pointed it forward so she could slide her mouth down my shaft. "Start with the head and work your way down." I kept my hand on the back of her neck and guided her down my length.

Oh fuck.

My cock was huge for her mouth, but she opened her jaw wide so she could take me. The grooves of her tongue felt amazing against my shaft. The friction was perfect, and her saliva was more than inviting. "You want to go hard but not nick my dick with your teeth. If you do, it could take a while for me to get back up to the same level of hardness." I'd been nicked before, and while it was an accident, it was uncomfortable. It usually took me a few minutes to get really hard again.

She gripped my thighs and moved her neck back and forth, taking in my cock as far as she could before pulling out so she could get some air. She took in more than I expected, only missing a few inches because it wasn't physically possible to get the entire thing in her mouth.

I couldn't believe this was happening.

Kayden was on her knees and sucking me off.

And she was doing a fucking fantastic job.

"Look at me as you do it."

Her eyes moved up to my face as she continued to suck me off. Her tongue remained flat on the bottom so my cock had the perfect surface to rub against. Saliva leaked from her mouth because my cock took up so much space.

"You're perfect. Keep going." I thrust my hips into her and we moved together. I stopped giving her direction because I enjoyed her mouth so much. It was a great blow job, one of the best I'd ever had. Her lips were so soft every time my cock slid farther into her mouth, and I could feel her throat when I pushed all the way back.

I felt the sensation start deep in my balls. I knew what was coming, and I wanted to come deep in her throat because it was the perfect ending. But that was something only romantically involved people did. The polite thing for me to do was come into my hand.

But I really wanted to come in her mouth.

"If the guy isn't a dick, he'll tell you when he's going to come." I fisted her hair and continued to thrust into her mouth. "He'll want you to swallow, and if you really want to impress him, that's what you should do. But if you don't want to, just pull out and jerk me off onto your face." Her mouth was so warm and wet, and I didn't want to leave it. But I managed to pull out and cup my head with my hand as I jerked off the rest of the way.

Kayden pulled my hand away and shoved my cock back into her mouth. She looked up at me as she shoved my dick deeper into her mouth. She moved harder and faster, trying to get me off with a powerful orgasm.

"You want me to come in your mouth, baby?"

She nodded as she kept moving.

She was so fucking perfect. "Here it comes." I held on to the back of her neck as I kept thrusting. I hit my threshold almost immediately, hard because of her request. The sensation hit me like a freight train, and I came in her mouth with a loud moan. My fingers dug into her skin, and I emptied myself in the back of her throat, giving her every drop. I hadn't gotten laid in about a week, and this release was exactly what I needed. "Fuck." I finished giving her everything before I softened in her mouth. My eyes felt lidded and heavy, exhausted from that mind blowing pleasure she just gave me. I looked at her with new eyes, unsure if I was teaching her anything or if she was teaching me everything.

She pulled my cock out of her mouth then licked her lips.

My eyes snapped open. Was this really the woman I'd been friends with my entire life? Was this really the woman I hadn't noticed until recently?

"So…how did I do?"

Those pretty lips did a tremendous job on my cock. All I needed to do was give her a few pointers, and she figured out the rest on her own. She really didn't need me at all. Any guy in the world would kill to be sucked off like that. And when she swallowed my seed like she needed it…amazing. "You don't even need to ask."

***

"Rae is calling." Kayden picked up her cell phone from the coffee table.

"Shit." I immediately went into panic mode at the thought of being caught. After all the shit I gave her about Ryker, she would be livid if she knew I was fooling around with Kayden—even if I was just trying to help her. "Be cool, alright?"

She rolled her eyes at me. "You're overreacting."

"That woman is psycho. I swear, she has superpowers."

"Does not." She took the call. "Hey, girl. What's up?" She paused and listened to Rae over the line. "Yeah. Sure. I can meet you there in fifteen minutes."

My phone started to ring at that exact moment. "Fuck." I quickly grabbed it and hit the silence button, hoping Rae didn't hear it over the line. If she did, I would be a dead man. Not too many people had the Star Wars anthem as their ringtone.

Kayden paused again when she listened to Rae. "Just the TV. Yeah, I like Star Wars."

Shit, she did hear.

Kayden quickly wrapped up the conversation. "I'll see you in a few." She hung up.

I took the call because it was Zeke. "Shit, what do you want?" I had a nervous breakdown just thinking of the repercussions of my sister finding out what I've been doing in my spare time for the past two days.

"Dude, are you okay?"

"I'm fine," I said quickly. "Why?"

"Are you with Kayden right now?"

Fuck. Fuck. Fuck. "Why would I be with Kayden? The only time I see her is when we all get together. Like, I don't hang out with her. I mean, we're friends but we aren't close friends. And she's not my type. Blondes—gross."

Kayden shook her head at me then mouthed, "Chill."

"Uh…okay. Anyway, we're going down to the bar if you want to come. Rae just got off the phone with Kayden, and she said she's coming."

"I'm just leaving Mega Shake, so I'll be there in a second."

"You're at Mega Shake?" he asked.

"Yeah. Why?"

"It just sounds really quiet."

"Oh, I'm in an alleyway right now." God, I'm so bad at lying.

"Uh, alright," Zeke said. "You know, alleyways—"

"Are you a doctor or a detective? I'll meet you there in fifteen minutes." I hung up and shoved my phone deep into my pocket.

"Rex, you need to calm down."

"Rae heard my ringtone." I've had that same ringtone for years now. It was unmistakable.

"You're being way too paranoid about this."

"I just don't want Rae to give me shit. After the big deal I made about Ryker, she would be so pissed at me."

"Well, no one is going to find out. We can keep it between us. Besides, we're both adults and can do whatever we want. So just calm down." She walked into my chest and wrapped her arms around my neck.

Instantly, the affection felt nice. "Yeah…got a little carried away."

She looked up at me with her bright eyes, looking appetizing as hell. "Good. Now we can go."

"We can't go together," I said. "That will be way too obvious."

"We can say we bumped into each other on the way."

"No. Rae and Zeke are too damn smart."

She rolled her eyes. "Well, I'll leave now and you can leave whenever you grow a pair." She grabbed her purse then walked out, leaving me alone in her apartment. She was shy and vulnerable when it came to the two of us being physical, but then she showed a stronger side of herself, a powerful one. Sometimes I wondered if I really knew her.

Maybe I didn't.

***

I walked in fifteen minutes after Kayden.

They were sitting in a booth together, the girls on the left and Zeke on the right. He had a Guinness in front of him, the beer so black it looked like oil.

I got a beer from the bar then took a seat beside Zeke, doing whatever I could to look natural.

"Where have you been for the past two days?" Rae rounded on me immediately, getting under my skin like the annoying sister she was.

"Mind your own business. That's where I've been."

"As long as you're living under my roof, I'm entitled to that information."

"I've been working a lot. It's pretty much a brand new business. You don't understand with that tiny little brain of yours."

She stuck her tongue out at me.

"Good one…" I turned to Zeke so I could have a conversation with a smart person. "How was work?"

"Okay. I was tired all day because someone kept me up."

"Seriously?" I asked. "Ten thirty is late for you?"

"I'm usually in bed by ten," Rae said.

"Because you're a loser," I snapped.

"Me too," Jessie said. "I've got to be ready to go by 7:30 in the morning, so I usually have to wake up at five."

"I'm usually in bed by ten too," Kayden said before she sipped her wine.

I dropped my insults once I heard her say that. She just blew me less than an hour ago. I wasn't going to say a single thing to tick her off.

Jessie turned to Rae. "Is Ryker coming?"

"No," Rae said. "I don't see you guys enough anymore."

"We understand," Jess said. "If I had a scorching hot boy toy, I'd never see you either."

Zeke downed his beer then went to the bar to get another.

I knew exactly why he left so I went after him. "I thought you were moving past this?"

"I am." He waved down the bartender and ordered another beer. "But sometimes it gets under my skin—usually when I'm drinking."

"Seen Missy since?" We tag-teamed a few girls a while ago. I hadn't met up with my girl because I hadn't really thought about her. I had a feeling Zeke did the same.

"No. Not really my type."

"Yeah." Zeke usually liked good girls, the kind he could introduce to his parents. He liked messing around with the loose ones, but he never took them to dinner and a show.

And I never took anyone to dinner and a show.

"What about you?" he asked. "What tail are you chasing now?"

I forced myself not to look at Kayden. It was so hard not telling my best friend the truth. I told him everything, even details he didn't want to know about. Keeping a secret from him felt like a crime. I'd be hurt if he kept something from me. "Not chasing any right now. But maybe I'll find some sexy ladies at the bowling alley."

"Yeah…because that's where they spend their free time."

"Hey, it could happen. Like a hot chick bowling league."

Zeke finally smiled. "That would be pretty cool…"

"I'd watch all their games."

"Yeah, me too." He rested his elbows on the bar and took a look around. "So Groovy Bowl is still busy?"

"Insanely busy. I just hired three more people."

"Good for you."

"I'll have your money back in no time."

"Don't worry about it." He shook his head. "There's really no rush. I know you're good for it."

"Thanks, man."

A woman with dirty blonde hair stood on the other side of the room with two friends. She wore a black dress across her wide stomach. She was curvy, thick in the arms and the waist. Her eyes were on Zeke, and when she handed off her drink to a friend, I knew she had her eyes on the target.

"Babe coming this way."

"For you or me?" Zeke remained sly and didn't look.

"You."

She tapped Zeke on the shoulder and waited for him to turn around.

Zeke was the athletic type, spending his time biking and hiking on the weekends. He competed in three half marathons a year and went to the gym religiously. He grew his own vegetables in his backyard and was committed to a healthy lifestyle. Most of the women he dated were similar. This woman was a little different. She was thicker than the women he usually dated, and she didn't possess the athletic and slender physique. She was cute, but not fit.

"Hi, I'm Rochelle." She flipped her hair over one shoulder and leaned against the bar. She had a nice smile with perfectly straight teeth. Her skin was fair with a few freckles on her nose. She wore makeup, but very little.

"Hi. I'm Zeke." He extended his hand to shake hers.

"I'm sorry if you have a girlfriend, and I can only assume you do, but if you don't, I'd like to ask you out sometime."

I admired her courage. Not many women could walk across a room and ask out a total stranger. She did it with such confidence that it made me wonder where it came from. Zeke was extremely good-looking, not that I checked him out, and most women would be intimidated to go after him so vigorously.

I wasn't sure what Zeke's response would be. She wasn't his typical type, and he was still hung up on Rae. This woman definitely wasn't the fuck buddy type. She wanted dinner and flowers—the whole she-bang.

"I'd love to," Zeke said. "Are you free on Friday?"

I guess she was his type.

"Absolutely free." She pulled out her phone and got his number. "I'll see you then."

"I look forward to it."

She gave him another smile before she walked back to her friends on the other side of the room.

Zeke turned to me, a smug grin on his face. "Looks like I have a date on Friday."

"She seemed pretty cool. Not too many women would have the balls to do that."

"I know. I'm sure we'll have a good time."

"And you did say there was plenty of fish in the sea. Looks like you caught a swordfish."

"A swordfish?" he asked. "That's not even a sexy fish."

"But it's a big fish. Have you seen them? They're humongous." I realized exactly how my words could be taken, and it was in a way I didn't mean whatsoever. "Wait, I didn't mean it like that… I just meant they're really rare and big for a fish. That's all. Sorry, you know how I meant that, right?"

"Yeah, of course. You're an ass, but I know you aren't that kind of dick."

I breathed a sigh of relief when he believed me. "Maybe Rochelle will help you get over Rae once and for all."

"I sure hope so. I'm tired of feeling like this." A defeated sigh escaped his lips. "I'm tired of dating and sleeping around. I'm thirty years old, and I'm ready to settle down. I've got a house and a career…but no wife. Rae clearly isn't going to be that, so I need to find someone else."

"Someone better." Zeke was the best guy I knew, and he deserved someone who was equally amazing. "And you will, man." I clapped him on the shoulder. "Things are already looking up."

"Yeah, they are." He turned in his chair so he was facing me better. "Any special ladies in your bed lately?"

An image of Kayden on her knees with her mouth tight around my dick came into my mind. I would never forget that moment as long as I lived. My hand pulled her blonde hair back, and the saliva dripped from her mouth and onto my shoes. It was the sexiest blow job I'd ever gotten. She knew how to use that pretty little mouth of hers. "No, not this week."

"Maybe you'll meet someone tonight."

"Maybe." I glanced to the booth and saw Kayden sip her wine. Nearly half of the guys in the bar were staring at their table, at her specifically. Just an hour ago, she sucked me off, but she didn't need my help whatsoever. She attracted the right kind of attention all on her own. She didn't need me at all.

But I was enjoying myself too much to tell her that.

Chapter Six

Rae

"Seriously, when the hell are you moving out?" The second I walked in the door, the kitchen was a mess. The blender sat on the counter, stained with the protein shake Rex made hours ago. There was water all over the counter and the floor, and there was an empty milk carton lying in the center of the kitchen.

His voice came from the living room. "Nice to see you too. Tell me about your day."

"Why is there a milk carton sitting on the floor?"

Rex finally got off his ass and joined me in the kitchen. He wore his old ripped jeans and a red sweater. His face was shaven, something he didn't start doing until Groovy Bowl reopened. He was actually taking time to make his appearance look decent. "Huh?"

I pointed to the milk carton. "Why is there a random milk carton on the floor?"

He eyed it then shrugged. "Don't know."

"You don't know?" What kind of answer was that? "Did you use it to make your protein shake?"

He rubbed his chin. "Can't remember…"

I couldn't live like this any longer. "You need to move out. I'm being dead serious right now. You're getting paid now, and you can afford rent. If you stay here any longer, I might kill you. I'm not joking." I'd been living with a slob for too long, and I needed my space back. Ryker never came over because Rex was always here, and the apartment smelled like ass—and not because of Safari.

"You're really that mad over a milk carton?" He reached down and grabbed it. "Look, all taken care of." He tossed it in the garbage.

"Then why didn't you do that before I came home?" My head was about to explode.

"I didn't see it, alright?"

I stomped my foot. "How can you not see it?"

"What's your prejudice against dairy? Almond milk tastes like shit."

"Not the point, Rex." I dragged my hands down my face so I wouldn't snatch a steak knife from the drawer. "The kitchen is still a mess even with the milk carton put away."

"Look." He ripped off a few paper towels and dropped them over the puddles of water. Instead of wiping down the counters, he just let them sit there and absorb the mess.

"You're joking, right?"

"What?"

"Aren't you going to throw them away now?"

"I'm letting the towels do their job."

I couldn't believe I was related to this guy. "You're ridiculous, Rex. What are you going to do when you get married?"

"Married? I'm never getting married. I'm not even seeing anyone. Not anyone."

"I didn't say you're getting married tomorrow. But if anyone does agree to marry you, which I highly doubt, they aren't going to put up with this. How many times have I told you to clean up after yourself? I'm tired of walking into a battlefield of trash."

"You think anyone is going to marry you with that shrill voice?"

"He'll never hear it because I would never marry an ass!"

"The only guy who would marry you is a deaf guy. And maybe not even then."

I smacked my hand against his arm. "We're finding you an apartment."

"I'm not leaving."

"Excuse me?" He was getting out of here even if I had to drag him. "You don't need to live here anymore. You're making money now and can afford a decent apartment."

"I need to save money to pay you guys back. Remember?"

"I don't need the money that bad. I would much rather not get paid at all and you not live here."

Because if he kept staying here, I would murder him and not have a brother at all.

"Rent, utilities, and food really adds up. If I saved that every month, I could pay you guys back twice as fast."

I stomped my foot like a child. "I don't care about the money, Rex. I just want you out."

"I'll clean up, alright? Look." He grabbed all the paper towels and carried them to the garbage, but water leaked from the bottom of the pile and dripped all over the place. He tossed them in the garbage, where they would soak everything else inside. "There. I fixed it."

I stared at the line of water that went all the way through the kitchen. It was like a goddamn river. "Just forget it."

***

"Please. Please. Please."

Zeke's deep voice came over the line. "No. Sorry."

"Come on. I've lived with him for six months now. It's your turn."

"I'm not related to the guy, so I don't have to do anything."

"But he's your best friend." I sat on my bed with the phone to my ear. Safari sat beside me, his chin resting on my thigh. "You're always with him anyway."

"Yeah, but I know he's a nightmare to live with. I'm at your place all the time and see the fun you two are having." He chuckled into the phone.

"But your place is huge, Zeke. You would both have plenty of room."

"I worked my ass off for this house, and I'm not letting that wrecking ball demolish it. If he thinks you're anal about keeping your apartment clean, he's not going to like living with me. Besides, when I have dates over, they like hanging out the next day. We make pancakes and watch TV. I wouldn't be able to do that with Rex around."

"He'd stay out of your way…"

"We both know he would eat all the pancakes and hog the remote."

I knew he was right but admitting that wouldn't help my cause. "He won't move out because he's trying to save money to pay us back."

"Not surprised. He's determined to pay off his debt."

"Well, his nobleness is goddamn annoying."

He laughed. "It's only for a few more months, Rae. Then he'll be gone for good."

"Ugh. I'm starting to hate him."

"Yeah…I can tell."

I rubbed my temple to fight the migraine fast approaching. "Rex mentioned you have a date this weekend."

"Yeah, I met her the other night at the bar. She asked me out."

"That's cool. Where are you guys going?"

"I'm taking her to that new café downtown."

"The one with all the pretty birdcages?"

"Yep."

"That's a cute place. Any woman would like that."

"That's what I'm thinking," he said. "And if things go well, we'll be eating pancakes and watching TV the next morning."

"I would love to eat pancakes and watch TV. Ryker never does stuff like that."

"He doesn't cook?" he asked in surprise.

"No. In fact, I've never seen him use his kitchen."

"Weirdo. If a lady goes the extra mile, I always make her breakfast. I guess I'm a gentleman."

"So if she's bad in bed, she doesn't get anything?" That didn't sound gentleman-like to me.

"No…I always make them breakfast no matter what."

***

What's my girlfriend up to? Ryker used that term whenever the opportunity presented itself, either because he thought it would butter me up or he liked saying it.

Locked in my room.

That sounds like fun...

Rex is driving me crazy so Safari and I are in hiding.

In your own apartment? His sarcastic tone seeped through the screen.

I realized just how pathetic I was in that moment. *Yeah...*

Come over here.

No. I don't need your pity invite.

It wasn't a pity invite. I want sex.

How sweet...

The three dots appeared immediately. *Sweetheart, get over here. Or I'll come get you myself.*

I didn't want to be there any longer, and my stomach was starting to rumble. *Can Safari come?*

Always.

Then we'll be there soon.

***

The elevator doors opened and Safari and I walked inside. The scent of pine needles and his cologne immediately hit my face, and I felt like I was in a safe haven. This place was heaven in comparison to the hell I just left. "So beautiful…"

Ryker stepped out from the hall in gray sweatpants that hung low on his hips. He was shirtless, like he usually was anytime he was in the apartment. "Thank you. You look beautiful too." He wore a smug smile.

He knew exactly what I was talking about but I let it slide. "Thanks for letting us crash here. Even Safari was annoyed."

He wrapped his arms around my waist and kissed me softly on the lips. The touch was gentle and warm, removing the taint of my terrible afternoon with Rex. He made me melt into a puddle on the ground, and I was perfectly fine with being a mess on the floor. "You guys are always welcome here." He gave my ass a playful squeeze before he stepped away.

"Are you talking to me or my ass?"

He wiggled his eyebrows. "Both."

I removed Safari's leash so he could find a comfy spot on the couch to lie down.

Ryker grabbed my purse and set it on the table. "So, Rex is a pain in the ass, huh?"

"I asked him to move out but he won't."

"Why wouldn't he?" He stood in front of me, his arms across his powerful chest. "He's making money now, right?"

I rolled my eyes. "He wants to save more money to pay us back. I told him I don't care if he ever pays me back. I just want him to leave."

He chuckled. "What a nightmare."

"When I came home today, there was a milk carton sitting on the ground...just sitting there." I stared into his eyes and saw the humor rise in his irises. "Like, how the hell do you drop a milk carton on the floor and just keep walking? How?"

He shrugged, his lips stretched into a smile. "Was it empty?"

"I think so. But there was water all over the counters and the floor. When I told him to clean it up, he dropped paper towels everywhere and that was it."

"Really?"

"He said he wanted the towels to absorb the water." I rolled my eyes again. "He's the biggest dipshit on the planet. That doesn't even make sense. And then when he threw the towels in the garbage, he got water everywhere—again."

Now Ryker was struggling to stop himself from laughing.

"This all happened the second I walked in the door. And he had a dirty blender sitting on the counter collecting germs. Why doesn't he just move to a garbage dump? He would feel right at home there."

Ryker finally laughed. "How much longer will he be there?"

I shrugged. "A few months…maybe more."

"Well, why don't you and Safari spend more time here?"

"So my apartment can be demolished with trash?"

"That way you can have a break. I've got a nice kitchen, several bathrooms, a nice living room, and not to mention, I'm always clean. So you guys would feel right at home here."

He basically just offered me a million dollars. "I would love to but that's okay."

"Why not?" He stepped closer to me. "Stay here three days straight every week. It'll give you a nice break from Rex so you won't hate him so much."

"I don't want to cram your bachelor pad with panties and dog hair."

"I welcome the panties. And the dog hair is fine. I'll have Mindy clean the house more often."

"Mindy?"

"Housekeeper."

I'd never seen her before. "My problem with Rex shouldn't be your problem too."

"Did you ever think I'm taking advantage of your problem with Rex to get you over here more often?" He pressed his face to mine but didn't kiss me. The proximity was enough to make me quiver.

"No…"

"Well, I am. So please stay here."

"What about Safari? He might accidentally do his business in your apartment."

"I'll ask Mindy to let him out every day at lunchtime. Problem solved."

"She shouldn't have to do that…"

"She'll appreciate the extra pay. Don't worry about it." He grabbed me by the hand and pulled me along with him. "Let me show you something."

"Okay."

He walked in front of me, the tight muscles of his back rippling as he moved. Every detail was carved from stone, and he looked so beautiful it was painful. "I like your back."

He turned around, his eyebrow raised.

"I mean, the muscles of your back. They look really nice." I could usually give a compliment pretty well, but this time, it came out stupid.

He finally smiled. "Thanks, sweetheart." He gave me a quick kiss on the ear, somehow making it one of the sexiest kisses I'd ever had. He walked into his bedroom then approached one of his thick dressers. Everything in his apartment was made of dark wood, suiting his personality perfectly. "See this drawer here?" He pointed to the one on top. It was two feet wide and several inches deep. "This is yours."

"Mine?"

"Yeah. Put your stuff in here. I can give you another drawer if you need it."

"You've seen my room. There's no space for anything in there because I have so many clothes."

"Alright. You can have the one beneath it too."

"Seriously?" It was that easy to negotiate.

"Yep." He leaned against the dresser and watched my face for a reaction. "What do you think?"

I knew no other woman ever had a drawer in his dresser, so this moment was particularly profound. I had something no other woman ever had. I was special—different. "I think your offer is really sweet, and I love it."

"Good." He shut the top drawer. "Bring all your panties over."

"But we have one problem."

"Hmm?"

"Safari needs a drawer too."

He chuckled. "For all his dog toys?"

"Yeah." I was being dead serious, and I didn't think he understood that. "And he needs a place to put his bed when no one is home."

"This is one high maintenance dog."

"He's my best friend, not just a dog."

Ryker rolled his eyes but smiled at the same time. "How about we get him a basket to put all his things in—and the dog bed."

"Deal. I would offer you a drawer at my place, but you wouldn't want one right now."

"I will when Rex moves out. And I want a nice drawer, one at the top."

"Now look who's high maintenance."

He gave me that smoldering smile, looking sexy without even realizing it. "I guess I am."

"So, what do you want to do now?" I shut the drawer then leaned against it. "Want to watch a movie or play a game?"

He eyed the door and spotted Safari lying on the couch in the living room. He walked to the door and shut it before he sat at the edge of the bed. He leaned back on his elbows and crossed his ankles. "You know what I want to do, sweetheart. I saved you from that troll, and I deserve to be rewarded."

"Is that your motivation behind everything? Sex?"

He considered my words like he was truly thinking about them. "Actually, yes." He patted the mattress beside him. "Now get to it."

***

Staying at Ryker's for a few days was exactly what I needed.

The house was clean, Ryker didn't do annoying things to get under my skin, and I got to have great sex every night before I went to bed. The top floor of his building had extraordinary views of the city, including the Space Needle. The lights flickered through the window, making it seem like we were on top of the world. His bed was the most comfortable thing I'd ever slept on besides his chest, and his sheets were made for royalty. I would be lying if I said I didn't fantasize about living there permanently—as his wife.

Safari liked it too. He had a lot more space than he did at my apartment, and a park was right outside the building, so he could do his business. He slept at the edge of the bed and had more room on the king size mattress than the full size one at my apartment.

Neither of us wanted to leave.

I got to know Ryker in a way I didn't before. I got to see his habits and his routine. He got up every day at five in the morning to head to the gym. Then he showered, had a protein shake, and then went to work.

I couldn't get up at five with a gun pointed to my head.

When he got off work, he jogged around the park then showered again before he threw on a pair of sexy sweatpants and kept his chest bare. Then he made dinner, something light like grilled chicken and vegetables.

His extremely healthy lifestyle made me feel like a pig.

I was too lazy to get out of bed a second earlier than I had to, and my idea of breakfast wasn't a protein shake. It was usually an Egg McMuffin from McDonald's or a leftover slice of pizza. I worked out sometimes but only a few days a week—if that. And his idea of dinner repulsed me. I needed carbs and fat in order to be happy.

Ryker sat across from me at the dinner table. He ate his chicken and vegetables slowly, taking his time like he was savoring the meal. "How's your stay at Hotel Ryker going?"

"The hospitality is good. That gets five stars."

"What else?"

"The sex is good. That gets five stars too."

"Alright."

"And cleanliness gets a five star too."

"So I get a perfect score. Awesome."

"Actually...you get a zero for food."

He stopped eating and stared me down. "A zero? You don't like my cooking?"

"Your cooking is fine. But when I opened the freezer, there was nothing in there."

"So?" His powerful shoulders coiled and moved every time he took a bite. The muscles of his body fused together so flawlessly it was hard to believe his physique was real. He looked like a model from an ad. "I don't eat anything from the freezer."

"No ice cream? No popsicles?"

"That's not food."

"Not food?" I asked incredulously. "That's absolutely delicious."

He chuckled. "I've never been a sweets kind of guy."

"And the only things in your fridge are meat and vegetables."

"Your point?"

"There're other food groups too. Like, you don't even have a carton of orange juice. Every person in America has a carton of orange juice in their fridge."

"It's full of sugar. And like I said, I don't like sweets."

"I couldn't live like this permanently. Next week, I'm stopping by the grocery store and getting normal people food."

He drank his wine and masked the smile on his face. "Staying in shape isn't about working out around the clock. It's about what you eat. And I'm very picky when it comes to putting food in my body."

"I'd rather have some fat on my body than be miserable all the time."

"I'm not miserable."

"I don't believe you." He ate a protein shake for breakfast, a banana for lunch, and meat and vegetables for dinner. I'd die if I did that every single day.

"What's real food to you?"

"Cheetos. Those are awesome. Macaroni and cheese. That shit is the bomb. Cheese quesadillas with some guacamole." My stomach rumbled just thinking about it. "Top Ramen and Rice-A-Roni."

"When you talk about food, you sound hard up."

"Because I am. You eat to live, and I live to eat. That's the difference between you and me."

"In that case, I'll make sure Mindy gets everything on your list. I want you to be full and horny."

"Perfect." I ate the rest of my dinner to be polite, but having it three nights in a row was getting old. It was fine if Ryker was committed to a life of healthy eating, but I would never conform to that lifestyle—ever. "When my belly is satisfied, I'll make sure you're satisfied too."

***

We sat on the couch together snuggled under a blanket. I hadn't removed my makeup once since I shacked up with him. He'd never seen me not wearing any, and I was a little self-conscious about it. Normally,

I wouldn't be. But Ryker was perfect around the clock, and I wanted to be too.

I rested my head on his shoulder with my arm wrapped around his waist. Even when he was sitting, his stomach was flat like a slab of concrete. I inhaled his scent and didn't pay much attention to the TV because I was treasuring him instead.

The night when I flipped out over Ryker's behavior, I knew I was in deep shit. This whole time, I thought I had a healthy attitude about our relationship, but I realized it was sucking me in like a black hole. My heart was growing more attached the longer we were together, and I knew falling for him was simply inevitable.

And I was pretty sure I already did.

He turned my way and brushed his lips across my temple. Lightly, he pressed a kiss against my warm skin. The affection was delicate and gentle, not aggressive and sexual like it usually was. When I stayed with him for any real duration, we did other things besides sex. We talked, watched TV, and played board games. He felt more like a boyfriend than he ever did before.

"I don't want you to go back home tomorrow." He kissed me again, right at the hairline.

"I don't either." I loved watching him shower every morning, the beads of water running down his ridiculously hot body. I loved hearing the alarm go off so we could have a quick fuck before he went to the gym. I loved walking through the front door and seeing him play tug-o-war with Safari in the living room. "But I need to."

"No, you don't."

"I have to check on my apartment. It could be in ruins by now."

"Oh well. You lost your security deposit."

If I had it my way, I would stay. But I didn't want to overstay my welcome and have him get tired of me. I knew he was the kind of man who needed his personal space. I didn't want to push him even though he thought he wanted to be pushed. "I lost it when Rex tried to fix the sink and made a huge hole in the wall."

He pressed his face into my neck and gave me gentle kisses. "Come on, sweetheart."

It would be so easy for me to fold. But I had to stay strong. "I'll be back again next week. And you know I'll see you in the meantime."

He breathed a sigh of defeat against my skin. "Alright. You win."

"I always win."

He grabbed my chin and directed my gaze on him. He stared into my eyes for a second before he pressed his mouth against mine. He gave me a slow kiss, the kind that was so good my thighs ached. It was full of passion and longing, like he never wanted to let me go.

I was in deep and there was no going back.

Chapter Seven

Rae

"Sorry, do I know you?" Rex looked at me from the couch with a beer in his hand. Zeke was sitting beside him watching the game on TV. Rex shaded his eyes with his hand and squinted. "I don't recognize you."

"Shut the hell up." I dropped my bag on the ground.

Safari ran over to Rex and licked his face.

"Don't worry, man." Rex gave him a good rub down. "I could never forget you. But that lady you walked in with...don't have a clue who she is."

I ignored the jab and sat on the other couch. "It's good to be home..." My sarcasm was heavier than rain from a storm. "I'm surprised the place isn't in shambles. I really thought your boxers would be all over the place."

"I'm not as messy as you make it sound," Rex argued.

"A damn milk carton in the middle of the kitchen." I turned to Zeke. "Do you have milk cartons hanging out on the floor?"

Zeke smiled then took a drink of his beer. "How was Hotel Ryker?"

"Really nice," I said. "He keeps his milk carton in the fridge."

Rex didn't crack a smile. "You're doing this every week now?"

"As long as you're still living here." I couldn't share a bathroom with him much longer. When I got up to go to work last week, Rex had already demolished the kitchen and eaten all the bagels. He was the biggest pain in the ass.

"At least you know he really likes you," Rex said. "I would never offer that to any girl I've ever dated."

"Me neither," Zeke said. "Except Rochelle."

"Oh yeah," I said. "How did your date go?"

"Great." He smiled from ear to ear, truly seeming happy. "We went out on Friday and had a great time. She slept over and stayed until Monday morning."

Rex gave him a high-five. "Sex-a-thon. Awesome."

"She was at your place the entire time?" Ryker didn't invite me to stay over until we'd been dating for two months. Zeke invited Rochelle over immediately. She must be really cool.

"Yeah." Zeke took another drink of his beer. "It kinda just happened. We had a great time on Friday then went bike riding on Saturday. Got some dinner. Then she came over again and we got down to business. On Sunday, we watched football all day. On Monday, she had to go home because she had work."

"Damn," Rex said. "Your dick must hurt."

"Nah," Zeke said. "She's a pro."

"Where does she work?" I asked.

"She's a pediatrician," Zeke answered. "She works at the hospital down the street, actually."

"Seriously?" Rex asked. "What are the odds she would be a doctor too?"

Zeke shrugged. "Crazy, huh? Like dissolves like."

"Huh?" Rex asked.

It was a scientific term we learned in chemistry. It wasn't surprising that Rex didn't understand it. "It just means things that are similar go well together."

"You mean, go good together?" Rex challenged.

Why did I bother? "That's great, Zeke. She sounds like a catch."

"Totally," Zeke said. "We should all go out together so you can get to know her better."

"Is that where this is going?" I asked. "In the relationship direction?" Most of the time, Zeke had flings. We saw the girl once and she never made another appearance. But sometimes he would have short-term relationships. This one seemed different than all the others.

"Yeah," Zeke answered. "We're already exclusive, so I would say so."

Damn, she had game. It took me forever to get Ryker to call me more than a friend. "Cool."

"What about you and Ryker?" Zeke asked. "Sounds like things are getting serious."

I would normally spill my every thought and feeling to Zeke, but it was just strange with Rex there. "I'm not sure. He gave me a drawer at his place and lets Safari stay there, so I think that's the direction we're going."

"That's more than he's given any other woman," Zeke said. "I'd say Ryker will be around for a long time."

There was nothing I wanted more, and I hoped he was right on the money.

***

"So you stayed at Ryker's for three whole days?" Jessie asked in surprise. She wore a low-cut top with skinny jeans and heels. Her hair was done so well it could have been her wedding day. She sipped her cosmo then set it on the table.

"That's a lot of sex," Kayden said. "Like, a lot."

"But it's never enough when it comes to Ryker." I saw their faces soften like my words were deeply romantic.

"Does this mean anything?" Kayden asked. "Do you think he'll ask you to move in with him?"

"I don't know," I answered. "When I had to leave, he asked me to stay…"

"This is getting really serious," Jessie said. "He went from wanting a one-night stand to making you his girlfriend and giving you a drawer. For a guy that doesn't do relationships, that's a pretty big deal."

"I know." It was almost too good to be true.

"You're the woman who changed him," Kayden said. "Like in all those romance movies."

"It's only a matter of time before he asks you to move in," Jessie said. "I can feel it."

"What would you do if he asked?" Kayden asked.

"I really don't know." I looked down into my drink and tried not to smile as I thought about it.

Jessie caught the look. "You know exactly what you would say."

"Yeah," Kayden said. "It's pretty obvious."

I looked up and didn't mask my grin. "Yeah...I probably would. I haven't felt this way about a guy in a really long time. I'm just...I don't know."

"Head over heels in love with him?" Jessie pressed.

"No..." I couldn't admit to myself I was there. If I did, my heart would explode. I hadn't been dating him that long, and just the fact that I had to stop myself from making that last leap told me this was serious.

Kayden looked at Jessie. "She does."

"I know." Jessie upturned her nose in the air like the little know-it-all she was.

I didn't waste my time arguing with them. "Since I stayed there for so long, we did things we've never done before."

"Like anal?" Jessie asked.

"No," I said quickly. "Like, we watched TV, played cards, cooked dinner together. You know, like married couple stuff."

"And?" Kayden asked.

The simple tasks touched my heart like nothing else ever had. "It was just as good as the sex."

"Awe," Kayden whispered.

"You got it bad," Jessie said. "But you know what? He does too. It's obvious."

I knew he cared about me. He wouldn't have stayed with me this long if he felt otherwise. I just wondered if he felt the way I did. Maybe he just wasn't ready to say it. "I've never been so jealous in my life. Last week, when I saw that hooch practically on his lap, I flipped a switch. I wasn't myself at all."

Jessie and Kayden both listened to me, hanging on to every word.

"It hit me then how I felt about him. In the moment, it felt like the end of the world." I could continue to mask my feelings, but it would only last for so long. A part of me wanted to tell Ryker how I felt and hear him say it back so we could move forward. I didn't need to get married or even move in together. But I just wanted him to know how I felt, that I was so hung up on him that I couldn't picture myself with anyone else for the rest of my life.

Shit, that's scary.

Jessie turned to Kayden. "Are you seeing anyone?"

"No." Her answer was so quick that it was awkward.

"Nobody?" Jessie asked incredulously. "You aren't even talking to someone?"

"Well, there's this guy I've been kinda fooling around with," Kayden said. "But it's more of a booty call situation."

"Is he hot?" Jessie said.

Kayden nodded her head dramatically. "The sexiest guy I've ever been with."

"Damn," I said. "Maybe you should make something more serious happen."

"We'll see," she said non-committedly. "He's not really the commitment type."

"None of them are until they meet the right gal," Jessie said. "I've been single for a while. Haven't found anyone interesting."

Sometimes I forgot she tried to hook up with Ryker. It seemed like a lifetime ago now. "Zeke is seeing some woman now. Seems like they hit it off."

"Good for him," Jessie said. "He's such a catch. If I didn't see him like a brother, I'd make a pass at him."

"Me too," Kayden said. "He's so sweet and smart…"

"Yeah, he's pretty perfect," I said. "I hope she's perfect too."

"I'm sure she is," Jessie said. "Zeke isn't really the relationship guy either unless the woman is exceptional."

"I'm not sure why my brother is such a screw up," I said. "You'd think Zeke would rub off on him."

"Rex is perfect the way he is," Kayden said. "You're just bitter because he's driving you crazy. He did a great job taking care of you, and he's working his ass off at that bowling alley. Don't you forget it."

Jessie stared at her with wide eyes.

I was just as surprised.

"Damn," Jessie said. "Someone's protective…"

"I'm just saying…" Kayden masked her awkwardness with a drink. "I know he can be annoying but he's definitely not a screw up. Just because Zeke is a doctor doesn't mean he's better than Rex. They're both great."

I thought it was weird she defended Rex so viciously when she knew I was just annoyed with him. As his sister, I could say whatever I wanted about him. Everyone knew I loved him regardless. Jumping to his aid so quickly when he wasn't even there wasn't really her style. But I didn't overanalyze the situation. "So I'm not sure what to do about Ryker. I guess just coast."

"Yeah, see where it goes," Jessie said. "You guys are in a great place anyway so just enjoy it."

"When he's ready to move forward, he'll tell you," Kayden said. "He's given you so much already that I think it's safe to say he's going to be around for a while."

"Yeah." I smiled at the thought. "I think you're right."

Chapter Eight

Rae

Ryker pinned me to his bed the second I walked through the elevator. He held himself over me, his naked body all hard muscle with a throbbing cock. His biceps tensed as he held his weight effortlessly. "I missed you."

My hands wrapped around his wrists, feeling his strong pulse race through his veined forearms. "I missed you too."

I was wearing a dress, so he moved his hand up my dress and pulled down my thong. It slid down my legs until it rested around one ankle. Instead of removing it, he left it there. Then he pressed his hips between my thighs and shoved himself inside me. "But my cock missed you more." He slid through my slickness with ease, drenched in my arousal. "I can tell the feeling is mutual." He slid through my wet tightness and groaned with pleasure.

My knees were pressed against my ribs, and I was balled into a tiny form while he thrust into me from above. He pushed me into the mattress every time he shoved his dick inside me. The headboard rocked against the wall, and all I could do was lay there and enjoy the sight of him fucking me hard. "Ryker..." My hands moved up his chest and to his shoulders. I dug my nails into his skin because I knew he liked it.

He pressed his mouth to my ear. "You like it when I fuck you like this?"

My nails dug into him again for an answer.

He slammed into me harder, hitting me so deep he was practically smacking into my cervix. He wasn't just long, but thick. Even after all this time together, he still stretched me in the most exhilarating way. I'd never felt so full with another man. "Your pussy is so tight no matter how many times I pound it." He groaned into my ear again and kept going.

I dragged my nails down his back until I reached his ass. His cheeks were all hard muscle, and I loved latching on to it so I could pull him deeper and harder inside me. "Harder. I'm gonna come."

"Yes, sweetheart." He gave it to me as hard as he could, making me bounce on the mattress because he was slamming into me so forcefully. His cock hit me hard every time, giving it to me good.

That was exactly what I needed, and I soared over the edge with a scream. "God, yes…" My head rolled back, and I closed my eyes as the sensation overtook me. Ryker gave me such amazing sex, and I was addicted to the nights we spent together in his bedroom. He satisfied me in ways no other man ever did. But yet, I still wanted more.

"That's my girl." He panted above me, his body covered in sweat.

"I want you to fill me." I pulled him harder inside my body, loving the look on his face when he came inside me.

His eyes darkened in desire. He lengthened his strokes, penetrating me longer and harder.

"Give it to me, Ryker."

"Fuck, sweetheart." He pressed his face to mine and gave me a hard kiss just before he came. "Fuck..." He rammed himself deep inside me, squirting his seed as far as it would go. He wanted to make sure my pussy took every single drop.

I pulled him harder into me, loving the feel of his softening dick once he was satisfied. "It's heavy... I can feel it."

He stayed above me and looked at me with those sex-drunk eyes. "You make me come a lot." He kissed the corner of my mouth before he slowly pulled out of me, my lubrication forming a sticky line as we separated. He reached between my legs and felt his come drip out. He let it stick to his fingers before he left the bed and walked to the bathroom to retrieve tissues.

I laid there and waited for him to return, wanting to have another round before dinner. When I was with Ryker, I didn't care about food or water. All I cared about was him deep inside me every single minute of the day.

***

Ryker lay next to me in bed, the clock on his nightstand displaying the midnight hour. He was usually asleep by this time since he got up at the crack of dawn, but he was still wide awake. He turned on his side and stared at me, his eyes unreadable.

"What?"

"I can't look at you?"

"You can. Just curious as to why."

"Because I enjoy it." His hand snaked across the sheets until it rested along the curve of my side. His five o'clock shadow had grown in, and now it was thick and ready to be shaven off. "Since you're my girlfriend, I can do whatever I want."

"You're getting fond of that title, aren't you?"

"Maybe I just like taking advantage of the label. It allows me to get away with more things."

"Such as?"

"Staring at you, for one. And teasing you, for two."

"True. You do like to tease me."

Safari lay at our feet, so Ryker had to bend his knees in order to move closer to me. "My favorite hobby."

I ran my hand along his chest and felt the scorching warmth that radiated at all times of the day. He was my personal heater in the cold city of Seattle. I didn't need central heating when I had him. "How's your father?"

His eyes narrowed at the sudden change in subject. "Why?"

"You never talk about him. How's he doing?" He said goodbye to me when he retired, but I hadn't heard from him since. I wasn't even sure if Ryker told him we were seeing each other.

"He's fine." It was a short answer, and it was clear I wasn't going to get more out of him.

"What has he—"

"I don't want to talk about him. Not now. Not ever."

I froze at the cold response, having no idea where it came from. He didn't talk about his dad much, and when he did, he didn't have much to say. But I didn't realize they had beef between them. Now I was even more curious, but I knew Ryker didn't want to discuss it. "There is one thing I want to know, and I'm entitled to ask it."

He gave me the same look of frost.

"Does he know we're seeing each other?"

His jaw was clenched like he might not answer. "No."

If his dad didn't know, his mom probably didn't either. I didn't know much about his family because he never mentioned them. Since his dad was so sweet and generous, I couldn't imagine why Ryker would have such a problem with him. But I guess there was more to the story.

***

"There they are." Rex stood up and waved Zeke and Rochelle over.

We were sitting at the lanes, wearing bowling shoes and listening to the balls collide with the pins on the other side of the room. Music from the 60's and 70's blasted overhead.

Zeke and Rochelle walked over hand in hand. She had dirty blonde hair that was more brown than blonde, and she wore jeans with a baggy shirt. The only women I'd seen Zeke with were supermodels. While Rochelle was pretty, she wasn't exactly what I was expecting. But since he wore a huge grin on his face and looked at her like she was a diamond in the rough, then she must be exactly what he wanted.

"Hey, guys." Zeke stopped when he reached us. "Rochelle, you already know Rex."

Rex pulled her in for a hug. "Nice to see you again. Zeke talks about you all the time." He gave her a thumbs up. "He says the sex is great."

Zeke immediately shot him a glare.

Instead of being uncomfortable, Rochelle laughed. "Good to know."

Zeke pulled her away before Rex could say anything else. "These are some of my friends. This is Jessie."

Jessie shook her hand. "Hey, girl. It's great to meet you."

"You too." Rochelle was all smiles, looking like a woman with a great attitude and zest for life.

I was the total opposite. My personality was built on sarcasm.

"This is Kayden." Zeke moved down the line.

Kayden shook her hand. "Welcome to the gang. We're going to get on your nerves fast."

Rochelle laughed again. "That's okay. I'm a little annoying too."

Zeke faltered when he came to me, looking a little awkward. "And this is Rae."

Rochelle looked me up and down, and it was the first time she didn't smile. In fact, she looked disappointed. Quickly, she recovered and adopted a smile but it wasn't as bright as it was a second ago. "It's so nice to meet you." She shook my hand.

Maybe I imagined that moment of hesitance from both of them. I hadn't pissed off Zeke lately, and there was no way I could have ticked off Rochelle that fast. It had to be all in my head. "You too. Zeke talks about you all the time." I glared at Rex. "And not just about the sex."

"Oh good," Rochelle said with a chuckle. "I'm glad he has more to say about me."

Zeke hooked his arm around her waist. "Where's Ryker?"

"He'll be here soon. You know him, likes to make an entrance to everything."

Zeke smiled. "He sure does. But we're going to have uneven teams."

"I suck at bowling," Jessie said. "So I really don't count."

"That's true," Kayden said immediately.

"Hey." Jessie turned on her at the betrayal.

"What?" Kayden said with a shrug. "It is. And I'm not much better."

Jessie's venom died away when Kayden threw herself under the bus too. "So, we're good."

"Is Ryker a good bowler?" Rex asked.

I shrugged. "How would I know?"

"Uh…because you're sleeping with him?" Rex raised an eyebrow.

"Yeah, because we do a lot of bowling while we're having sex," I said like a sarcastic smartass.

Rochelle immediately laughed at my joke.

Zeke looked down at her with fondness in his eyes.

Rex looked like he wanted to kill me. "When is he gonna get here?"

"When he gets here," I snapped.

"I'm gonna throw a ball at your head," he threatened.

"Like you could pick it up, little girl." I put my hands on my hips and challenged him. Staying with Ryker a few days a week had subdued my rage, but I was still ticked at my brother.

Zeke leaned toward Rochelle. "Siblings…"

"Oh," she said. "I thought they might be exes."

"Gross!" Rex jerked in disgust. "Hell no. I'd have sex with Zeke before that happened."

"Me too." I didn't realize what I said until it was too late. But when I looked at Rochelle, she didn't seem upset. In fact, she was chuckling at our little fight.

Jessie eyed the time on the clock. "Hope Ryker gets here soon. Otherwise, this argument is going to last a while."

"There he is." Kayden pointed to the entrance.

Ryker walked inside in jeans and a gray V-neck. He wore a leather jacket, the first time I'd ever seen him wear one. He looked around the lanes to find us, looking like a model cut out from a catalog. His face was cleanly shaven, and his dark hair was still perfect from styling it that morning before work. Every woman nearby turned their heads in his direction, practically snapping their necks.

Nope, bitches. He's mine. "Babe." I waved my hand in the air so he would spot me. I'd never called him that before, and it just came pouring out. While I wanted to get his attention, I also wanted everyone to know that fine piece of man meat was mine.

His eyes landed on me, and a small smile stretched across his face. He grabbed his bowling shoes from the counter then walked over to us. He nodded to everyone in greeting and went right for me. His hands slid around my waist and he pressed his face close to mine. "Babe?"

"What? People call each other that."

"You never call me that." He gave me a small kiss on the lips, more of a tease than anything else. "What's that about?" He smiled like he already knew the answer.

"A bunch of hoochies were checking you out. Just wanted them to know you're off the market."

"Hoochies?" Both of his eyebrows shot up. "I haven't heard that word since seventh grade."

"Well, it's a good word. Never should have died out."

He rubbed his nose against mine. "I like it when you're jealous. It's hot."

"Yeah?" I thought it was just pathetic. I got jealous at the bar, and then I got jealous again just because a few women looked at him. I used to make fun of people for acting that way, but now I was doing it on a regular basis.

"Oh yeah." His hands snaked down to my ass and he gave me a firm squeeze. "Your cheeks get all red, and you get a bossy attitude. I like it when you're insecure because you're never insecure. It's a new side to you."

"You get jealous too."

"I know." He squeezed my ass again. "But I actually have a reason to be jealous." He kissed my neck before he turned away and greeted my friends properly. "Who's this?" He walked up to Rochelle and extended his hand.

"I'm Rochelle." She beamed at him even brighter than everyone else.

"My girlfriend," Zeke explained.

It was the first time Ryker truly smiled that day. "That's great to hear. Good for you, man." He dropped her hand then sat on the bench to put on his shoes. "Whose team am I on? I don't care as long as I'm not on Rae's."

"Ouch," I barked. "What did I do to you?"

"Nothing." He tied his shoelaces before he stood up. "I know you hate to lose, and I want to put you in your place. You know, show you who's boss."

"I'm warming up to this relationship..." Rex walked to the monitor and began to put our names in.

He greeted me with such affection then he turned on me. "I'm gonna kick your ass. And when I do, I'm not putting out. That will put you in your place."

Ryker laughed like the threat was absolutely ridiculous. "Okay, sweetheart. Whatever you say."

"What?" I put my hands on my hips. "You don't think I can beat you?"

"No. I just don't think you can keep your legs closed."

"Ooh…" Jessie covered her mouth and tried not to laugh.

Kayden shook her head. "Burn."

Rex just covered his ears.

Zeke pulled Rochelle tighter into his side. "Told you my friends were nutcases."

"It's okay," she said. "I'm a nutcase too."

***

My team consisted of me, Zeke, Rochelle, and Kayden. Kayden was dead weight and just rolled gutter balls, but Zeke and Rochelle were both pretty good. Rochelle was surprisingly awesome. When I asked if she bowled regularly, she said she was on a charity team for the hospital she worked at.

At the end of the game, we won by a few dozen points.

I walked up to Ryker full of attitude and started my victory dance. I shook my hips and spun around, being as smug as possible. "Take that, smug prick."

He watched me dance in front of him, his eyes dark with their usual intensity. "Smug prick?"

"Yep. Looks like you lost to a bunch of girls."

"Eh-hem." Zeke stared me down with annoyance.

"And Zeke," I corrected. "Sorry."

Ryker snapped his fingers. "Keep dancing. It's pretty hot."

I smacked his arm. "I'm serious. I kicked your ass. How about that?"

He shrugged. "You want me to bow to you?"

"I want an apology."

"For...?"

"Saying you didn't want to be on my team."

"I'm not apologizing for that. I still don't want to be on your team."

"You think I want to use sex as a weapon?"

That same smile stretched on his lips. "When we get back to my place, you're going to be riding me within ten minutes."

"Alright...I'm going to the snack bar." Rex walked away, nearly running up the stairs.

"Me too." Kayden followed behind him, leaving Jessie with Zeke and Rochelle.

"Do they always fight like this?" Rochelle asked.

"Not sure," Zeke said. "But I know Ryker always teases her."

I crossed my arms over my chest. "Arrogance isn't sexy."

"Arrogance has nothing to do with it. I just know my woman." Ryker smiled. "And I know what she likes."

I forced myself not to melt when he referred to me so possessively. I kept my spine straight and didn't back down. "Well, I'm going home tonight. So good luck with that." I walked around him and chased after Rex and Kayden. I could use some good food.

Ryker spoke when he thought I was out of earshot. "By the end of the night, I'll have her on all fours."

***

We got dinner at the pizzeria. Ryker took the seat across from me and ate his slices slowly, his intense gaze glued to me the entire time.

I ignored him and talked with my friends. "Rochelle, you're a doctor too?"

"Yeah," she answered. "Pediatrician. I work with kids." She finished two beers and was on her third, keeping up her pace with the guys.

"You guys must have a lot to talk about then," I said. "That's cool."

"Well, we have really different scopes of practice," Zeke said. "They're really apples and oranges."

"Because you aren't a real doctor?" I teased.

Zeke rolled his eyes. "They think I just pop pimples all day."

Rochelle smiled. "You don't?"

"Ooh." Rex clapped his hands. "I like her, Zeke. She gives you shit like the rest of us."

Zeke glared at her in a playful way. "She does. But she makes it up to me when we're alone."

"Happily," Rochelle said.

I grabbed another slice and kept eating, ignoring Ryker's perpetual gaze.

"You look so sexy when you eat, sweetheart."

I kept my eyes down.

"I know I'm on the other side of the table," Rex said. "But I can hear you."

"Then get some earplugs," Ryker said.

Rex grabbed a piece of garlic bread and threw it at him. But it missed by nearly a foot.

"Throws like a girl…" I mumbled under my breath.

Rex threw another garlic stick that hit me right in the face. "Now look who's a girl."

I picked it up off the table and ate it. "Yum."

"God, you're gross," Rex said.

Ryker eyed me with the exact same expression. "I've always liked my women dirty."

Rex cringed then turned to Kayden. "Talk to me about something. Anything."

She told him about her day at the library and how they were reorganizing the shelves. Rochelle talked to Zeke about going hiking the next day, and Jessie jumped into the conversation and said she didn't own a pair of running shoes.

I kept my eyes on my food and ignored him.

"Tune me out all you want, sweetheart," he said. "But when we get home, it's on."

"That's what you think…"

Ryker stopped eating altogether and chose to occupy his time by staring at me. He sat with his elbows on the table, observing me like he was watching a film. He hardly blinked because he was so absorbed.

His tactics were already getting to me but I refused to cave. I purposely ate another slice just to avoid him.

"Ryker?" A beautiful woman came to his side at the table. She wore skinny jeans and a tube top, looking like she was going to the club rather than bowling. Her hair was done like she just stepped out of the salon. Judging by the way she looked at him, she'd already been in his bed long before I came along.

I refused to get jealous.

Wasn't gonna happen.

Don't care.

"How are you?" Her hand immediately went to his shoulder like she had every right to touch him.

Forget it. I'm jealous. Damn jealous.

"Good. What brings you here?" He turned his shoulders naturally, forcing her hand to slide off.

That's right.

"Some friends and I are out. Want to join us?"

She clearly thought he was just hanging out with a group of friends. Since my hair was thrown in a bun and I was stuffing my face with pizza, I obviously didn't look like Ryker's type. I couldn't blame her for thinking that. And I wasn't showing him an ounce of affection.

"Thanks for the offer," he said. "But I'm hanging out with my girlfriend and her friends."

I felt the thrill shoot down my body when he actually referred to me that way. I'd never heard him say it outside our group. And it was nice to hear—really nice.

"Oh..." She couldn't recover from her shock. Her eyes turned to me, and judging by the surprise I saw there, she wasn't sure if I was the girlfriend he was referring to—because I looked like a slob. "Oh, I'm sorry. Have a good night."

"I will," he said. "You too." He gave her a wave as she walked off.

Now it was hard to hold my grudge. He did exactly as I asked and wouldn't even let her touch him.

He turned back to me, the same look in his eyes as he had before. He only had his sights on me and nothing else.

My resentment was fading away, and I didn't care about the game we just bowled. I didn't care that he teased me in front of his friends. And I didn't care that he said I couldn't keep my legs closed when it came to him.

Because it was true.

He knew he had me right where he wanted me. That hint of arrogance was in his eyes. "You wanna get out of here?"

Chapter Nine

Rex

Jessie went home, but the rest of us came back to the apartment. I was glad Rae took off with Ryker. She'd be at his place until tomorrow afternoon. I wouldn't have to watch him stick his tongue down my sister's throat.

"Nice place," Rochelle said as she walked inside.

"Thanks." I grabbed a few beers and handed them out. When I gave one to Kayden, I did my very best not to touch her. If I did, I knew my cock would spring to life. She wore these skinny jeans that highlighted her perfect curves. And the t-shirt she wore hugged her glorious breasts. I hadn't seen her naked just yet, but my imagination painted a good picture.

"It's not his place," Zeke explained. "It's Rae's."

"You live with her?" Rochelle asked.

I'd been teased for this so many times I didn't feel any shame. "Yeah. Trying to save money."

"Oh, cool." Rochelle accepted my explanation without judgment and walked into the living room.

When she was out of earshot, I turned to Zeke. "She's really cool, man."

"I know." He grinned to himself before he twisted off the cap to his beer. "She really is."

"So...is Rae off your mind?" They'd only been seeing each other for two weeks, but their relationship was moving pretty quickly. He introduced Rochelle as his girlfriend, and he spent nearly all his free time with her. That worked out for me because I'd been seeing Kayden a lot more. If he were single, I'd have to make excuses not to hang out with him.

"I haven't really thought about her." Zeke spoke like he was talking to himself more than me. "So yeah, I think so."

"That's great."

"Yeah. It was never gonna happen with her anyway. If I told her how I felt, she would have just rejected me, and it would have made our friendship awkward. It worked out much better this way. Rochelle is really cool, sexy, funny, and smart."

I would never forget what Zeke had said to me about Rae, that he could see himself settling down and marrying her. If he was going to end up with anyone, it would be her. It wasn't something you would say if it was just a simple crush. He was downplaying it now, but that was fine. Rochelle was a much better fit, and she would be good to him. Rae had her priorities wrong. She wanted to chase a heartless bad boy until he kicked her to the side.

I could admit Ryker had been around a lot longer than I expected him to be, and they did seem close. But I hadn't changed my prediction. In a few months, he would get tired of her and move on to someone else. Rae would come home crying and expect me to put her back together.

But I would say I told her so.

"She's perfect, man. I hope it works out."

"Me too. That house is too big for one person."

"Well, I could fix that for you."

He chuckled. "No way. Rochelle walks around naked all the time. I'm not gonna lose that."

"I can walk around naked for you."

He rolled his eyes and walked away.

"Did you grow up in Seattle?" Kayden asked from the living room. She sat on one couch, and Rochelle sat on the other.

"Born and raised," Rochelle answered. "But I moved to California for medical school and my residency."

Zeke sat beside her and wrapped his arm around her shoulders.

I eyed the other couch where Kayden was sitting but didn't know what to do. If I sat there, it would seem like we were on a date or something. But if I sat next to Zeke and Rochelle, that would be a cramped fit.

Kayden watched me, waiting for me to do something.

Zeke noticed me standing there. "Everything alright?"

"Yeah," I said quickly. "Why?"

"You look weird standing there," he said. "Why don't you sit down?"

I eyed the seat beside Kayden before I took it. But I sat all the way to the left and nearly off the edge.

"Does Kayden smell?" Zeke asked with a chuckle.

"No." I rested my arm on the armrest and tried to look casual. "Better angle for the TV."

Zeke dropped the interrogation when he realized the conversation wasn't going anywhere.

Kayden eyed me from her seat on the couch, looking absolutely fuckable in her jeans and t-shirt. Even when she wasn't dressed in heels and a mini skirt, she looked phenomenal. I've known her for over ten years and not once did I look at her like this. But now, I couldn't stop thinking about it. She sucked my dick like a pro, and I wanted her to do it again.

"Want to play a game?" Zeke asked. "How about Cranium?"

"No," I said quickly. "You guys are way too smart for us. How about poker?"

"That's a guy's game," Zeke said. "Monopoly?"

It was long and boring but whatever. Maybe it would distract me enough to stop thinking about Kayden riding my dick like a goddamn cowgirl.

***

Zeke and Rochelle left after midnight, and Kayden lingered behind.

I hoped she would stick around, but I also wanted her to leave. Rae could come home at any second, and I'd have a very difficult time explaining why Kayden and I were alone in the apartment—naked.

"Are you going to take off too?" I stayed by the door so I could let her out.

She tucked her luscious blonde hair behind her ear, her eyes sparkling like stars. "I was hoping I could stick around, if that's okay. You haven't given me a new lesson in a while."

My dick was already hard. "Rae could come home at any moment..."

"Believe me, she's not. Did you see the two of them over dinner?"

I tried to block it out.

She stepped closer to me, her eyes glued to my lips. She sauntered in a sexy way, looking like a fantasy I'd beat off to on nights I was too lazy to pick up a date. When her chest was pressed to mine, she didn't touch me. She stared at me in her innately beautiful way, practically begging me to kiss her.

This woman had super powers.

I broke the tension and gripped her by the hips. My mouth found hers, and I kissed her hard. I turned her around and pressed her into the counter. The second our mouths were locked together, I fell hard into the abyss of carnal desire. I'd kissed a lot of women, but none of them had the power she possessed. She made me warm from the inside out, made my dick harder than steel, and took my breath away all in a single instant.

My hands tightened on her hips, and I pressed my hard cock against her, out of control with longing. I sucked her bottom lip before I shoved my tongue into her mouth, feeling her desperate tongue dance with mine.

My head was in the clouds, and even if Rae walked in right then, I wouldn't stop. I kissed her jawline then her neck before I rose up to her ear. I nibbled on her earlobe then swiped my tongue across her shell. "What do you want to learn?"

She gripped my arms tightly. "Whatever you want to teach me."

I wanted to teach one thing in particular. I lifted her by the ass into my arms and pulled her against my chest. My mouth sealed over hers as I carried her into my bedroom. Safari lay in the hallway and ignored us as we walked by.

When I was in my bedroom, I kicked the door shut behind me and dropped her on my bed. "If you're with a good guy, he'll do some serious foreplay—as he should." I kissed her as I undid her jeans and pulled them down her thighs. She helped me kick them off until she only had on her thong.

She pulled her top off on her own, and I reached behind her back and unclasped her bra. Like moving water, we worked together effortlessly to get what we wanted. She didn't seem awkward or inexperienced at all. In fact, she was one of the best lovers I'd ever had.

When her bra was gone, her tits were on display. I wanted to stare at those perky breasts but I wanted to kiss her more. My fingers found her panties, and I pulled them down her legs, excited to know that she was about to be completely naked underneath me.

I broke our kiss and finally looked down at her, knowing I crossed a line I could never uncross. We could return to just being friends when this was over, but I would never look at her the same. I would always picture her naked every time I saw her. "Shit, you're perfect." She had a narrow waist, nice hips, and a boobalicous chest I would love to tit fuck. My hands moved to her slender waist, and I gripped her harder than I meant to. I was so eager to feel her that I couldn't think. I stilled for a moment because I couldn't decide what to do next. Too many things hit me at once, and I lost control.

Her hands gripped the end of my shirt and pulled it over my head, bringing me back to earth. She tugged it off until my chest was visible for her to see. She tossed it on the ground then ran her hands up my body. "You're the one who's perfect, Rex." She looked at me with those big gorgeous eyes and her nails sank into my skin. Somehow, she seemed to want me more than I wanted her—which I didn't think was possible.

She moved for my jeans next and got them off, along with my boxers. When I was naked, I moved on top of her and pressed my cock against her stomach, unable to believe this beautiful woman wanted me—trusted me.

"Are you sure you want to do this?" It was stupid of me to ask. I was so turned on I couldn't have stopped if she asked me to. But the words flew out of my mouth, and I prayed she wouldn't change her mind.

"Yes." She kissed my neck and ran her fingers through my hair, her sexual intensity the same as mine.

"Our friendship will never be the same."

She kissed me again, harder. "We were never that close anyway."

I was done. I did the gentlemanly thing so I was out of the woods and guilt free. I grabbed her hips and yanked her to the edge of the bed. Her beautiful ass hung over and her legs were parted. My knees hit the carpet, and I pressed my face between her thighs. The second my mouth touched her pussy, she writhed.

"Oh god..." She gripped my sheets and arched her back.

My tongue circled her clit, giving her the perfect amount of pressure to make her moan from deep in the back of her throat. My tongue moved backward and forward, absorbing the sweet taste of her slick pussy. She was wet for me, and we hadn't even gotten started yet. She was doing a marvelous job, and I hadn't given her a single lesson. What the hell did she need me for?

I continued eating her out, getting her pussy soaking wet and prepared for my throbbing cock. I wanted to be inside her so bad but I paced myself. Nothing would make this night worse than if I came right when we started. I never had a problem stopping myself from blowing my load, but I suspected things wouldn't be easy with her.

I pushed her to the edge, right before she was about to come, and then I pulled my face away.

She sat up immediately, her eyes lidded with lust. "What lesson was that?"

"No lesson. Just want to make sure you know exactly how a man should eat your pussy." I grabbed her waist and tugged her back up the bed until I was on top of her. My hand shot to my nightstand and rifled in the drawer until I found a condom.

"I'm on the pill."

I held the condom in one hand and looked her in the eye. Was she inviting me to go bareback? We were just fooling around, so it was an intimate offer.

"Are you clean?" Her eyes looked hopeful.

"Yeah." I just got tested last week, actually.

"Then no condom."

Seriously? Kayden was going to let me fuck her skin-to-skin? No woman had ever made the offer before. "Are you sure? I can get my papers."

"I trust you." She cupped my face and kissed me. "I know you would never do anything to harm me."

The confession burned my heart as well as my dick, and now I was ready to fuck her pronto. My cock found her folds, and I slid through her slickness as I prepared to take the final plunge.

She dragged her nails down my back. "You have anything to teach me?"

I watched her tits shake as I rocked with her. "No. You're perfect."

She grabbed the base of my cock and pointed my head at her entrance. She used one of my shoulders as an anchor before she pushed me hard inside her. A moan escaped her lips when she felt the fullness.

Fuck, she was tight.

So goddamn wet.

Slick.

Warm.

Heaven.

"Fuck..." I closed my eyes to cherish the sensation. Now I understood why men skipped the condoms most of the time. Nothing compared to this, to feeling her wet flesh rub directly against mine. It was indescribable.

"God, you feel so good."

I didn't even need to tell her to say it. She was a natural.

Instinctively, I grabbed the back of her neck and held her in place as I fucked her hard. I gave it to her good and rough, my hips moving at lightning speed and my cock sliding through her abundant slickness.

She dug her nails into me harder. "Fuck yes."

Sweat drenched my back and my chest but I kept going. I pounded into her like it was the last thing I'd ever do. I hadn't had a lay quite this good in a long time—if ever. I wanted to go on forever, but I wanted to come even more.

I watched her tits shake as I thrust into her, her nipples hard and desperate to be sucked. Her chest was tinted pink along with her cheeks, but her eyes were just as bright as ever. Her hair stretched across the comforter, and she looked like an ultimate fantasy.

I grinded my hips against her and pressed right over her clitoris, wanting to get her off before I accidentally blew my load. My performance was never an issue, but I'd never been as hard up as this. The fact that she was my friend and taboo just got my engine going even more.

Thankfully, she did. "Right there…" She gripped my ass and yanked me harder into her. Her mouth opened and a sexy scream escaped her lips. Her pussy clenched around me, tightening until it constricted my cock with formidable force. Her pelvis bucked as the orgasm hit her hard, smacking into her like a train. "Yes…so damn good." She closed her eyes as she rode the high, enjoying every single second of her ecstasy.

How was I not supposed to come after that goddamn performance?

Her slickness overwhelmed my cock as her come surrounded me, and I could feel the thick stickiness her body produced just for me. She was smooth and wet, but she was also so viscous.

I wanted to keep going, but I knew that wasn't possible.

"My turn." She gripped my shoulder and rolled me onto my back.

This was too damn good to be true.

I lay on my back and watched her straddle me. Instead of pressing her knees to the bed, she balanced on the balls of her feet and gripped my tight stomach for balance. Like an athlete, she bounced up and down on my dick, her ass smacking my thighs every time she came down.

Was this really happening?

She took my dick like a pro and kept bouncing, burying my enormous cock deep inside her over and over. We were so wet together, and my thick cock opened her lips wide every time I thrust inside her.

I gripped my skull because I couldn't believe how good this was. "Fuck. Fuck. Fuck."

She rode me hard and sheathed my entire length to my base. She fucked my cock like she loved it more than anything else in the world. Her nails dug into me, and she moaned as she worked up a sweat, her tits shaking.

"I want to make you come again...but fuck...I really want to come."

"I want you to come too." She slowed down her pace and reached behind her ass, her fingertips finding my nuts. She massaged them gently as she continued to ride me up and down. The touch was magnificent, fucking incredible.

She didn't need me to teach her jack shit. "Baby, you're gonna make me come."

"I want you to come." She sheathed my entire length then circled her hips, keeping every inch inside her as she continued to rub my balls.

Pure heaven. That's what this was. I gripped her hips and thrust into her from underneath until my head exploded, and I pumped her with my seed. I moaned louder than I ever had during sex and drenched her pussy with my come. I'd never filled bare pussy before, and fuck, it was the best. "Oh my fucking god."

She leaned over me with her hair pulled over one shoulder. She looked down at me with an expression of pure satisfaction. Then she gave me a light kiss on the lips, like she didn't just fuck me like an animal.

She snuggled into my side, my come still deep inside her. She closed her eyes, and almost instantly, she fell asleep.

I did the same.

***

When I woke up, it was sometime late in the night. I wiped the sleep from my eyes and glanced at the clock sitting on the nightstand.

12:15 am.

We both slept longer than we meant to. I turned on my side to look at her, and I was surprised how pretty she looked when she was asleep. Her makeup was smeared, but somehow it looked sexy—like I gave her the time of her life. She was still naked, her nipples hard from the cold.

I grabbed the blanket and pulled it over both of us, covering her naked form from view.

She stirred at the movement. She stretched her body, straightening her legs and taking a deep breath. When she opened her eyes, they were full of both satisfaction and sleepiness. Her hand snaked across my stomach, her nails gently biting into me in an affectionate way. "I'm wiped out."

"Me too." I'd go back to sleep if I weren't so hungry. "So…do you have something to tell me?"

"What do you mean?"

"All that shit you said about being inexperienced was totally bogus."

She quickly straightened at the comment. "No…I'm just comfortable with you."

"I don't believe that. You climbed on top of me and fucked my cock like a porn star."

Now she furrowed her eyebrows in attitude. "Are you insulting me or complimenting me? Because I honestly can't tell."

"Complimenting. Always." I propped myself up on an elbow and looked down at her. "I feel like I'm taking advantage of you because you don't need any guidance. Honestly, I should be taking lessons from you. I've never had a girl fuck me that good."

Her mouth instantly formed a smile. "Really?"

"Yeah."

Her eyes lit up like a Christmas tree. "Well...thanks."

"So maybe we shouldn't do this anymore. I mean, it's great and everything. But it might get weird."

"Weird how?"

"Because we're friends."

Her happiness faded away. "I thought the sex was pretty incredible. You should give yourself more credit."

I released a sarcastic snort. "It's all you, sweetheart."

She ran her hand across my chest and looked at me with those beautiful eyes. "I don't want to stop…"

My cock hardened all over again. She was practically begging me, and that sounded so undeniably good. "I don't either." That was the best sex I'd ever had, and I never wanted it to end. I could do that every morning and every night.

"Then let's keep going."

"Baby, I have nothing to teach you. You can go out and bag any guy you want."

"But I want you." She gripped my shoulder and leaned her face close to mine. She stared at my lips like she might kiss me. Her long blonde hair fell over one shoulder, soft against my arm.

Now my cock wanted to be inside her all over again. "Then what is this?"

She shrugged. "A booty call situation."

"You want to be fuck buddies?" I didn't think Kayden would be interested in something like that. She was so quiet and kept to herself. I assumed she was looking for a Prince Charming and a happily ever after.

"Yeah. Why not?"

"Won't that mess up our friendship?"

"Not if we're both adults about it."

"So...we just hook up and keep it a secret?"

"Yeah."

"And then when one of us gets bored, we just stop?"

Her eyes shifted in a quick reaction, but she covered it up instantly. "Yeah."

My brain was warning me this was a bad idea. But my cock didn't want this arrangement to end. I didn't want to pick up some woman from a bar when I could just have awesome sex like that whenever I wanted. All I had to do was ask, and I would get it. "As long as we can go back to being friends afterward, I'm cool with it. And if we keep it a secret."

"Sounds good to me."

The decision had been made, and now it was time to take advantage of it. "I want to fuck you again, but damn, I'm starving."

"Me too."

"I'll get something from the kitchen. I'll be right back."

She pressed a kiss to my shoulder as I got up, and the small amount of affection was so sexy. It gave me chills down my spine.

I faltered for a moment before I kept going. I pulled on my sweatpants and walked into the hallway.

Then I came face to face with Rae.

"Who are you talking to?"

I froze on the spot and nearly jumped out of my skin. Safari was at her feet and she looked tired, like she should already be in bed instead of out in the hallway with me. "You?" My heart was beating so hard it actually hurt.

"Just a second ago."

Not only would it be awkward if Rae knew I was hooking up with Kayden, but it would make their relationship weird. "Aren't you supposed to be at Ryker's?"

"This is my place, nitwit. I can come and go as I please."

"Well, that's my room and what I do in there is none of your business."

"It is when I'm paying your rent," she snapped. "I don't care if you have a girl in there, but let me know so I'm prepared."

I crossed my arms over my chest and couldn't think of a damn thing to say.

"So…do you have a woman over?"

I walked around her and headed to the kitchen. "I'm starving."

"Aren't you going to make something for your date?"

I turned around. "Did Ryker kick you out because you're annoying as hell?"

She narrowed her eyes. "He kicked me out because he can't believe I'm related to such a turd." She finally walked into her room and shut the door, Safari accompanying her.

When she was out of sight, I finally took a breath. I wasn't even hungry anymore but I quickly made a sandwich just in case Rae came out again. It was the only time I did my best not to make a mess so she wouldn't pay more attention to me. I booked it back into the room and locked the door behind me.

Kayden was already dressed, so she must have overheard the conversation. "Shit."

"I thought she was going to stay at Ryker's tonight. Not sure what the hell happened."

"Damn." She crossed her arms over her chest. "Now what?"

"I guess you can sleep here and leave after she goes to work."

"I have to open the library tomorrow."

Did anyone really show up right when it opened? "Can you be a little late?"

"No."

"Who reads at eight in the morning?"

Now she gave me a pissed look that was strangely similar to the one Rae gave me. "A lot of people. Don't act like my job isn't as important as yours."

"Never said that. I just think you can be late one time."

"Not if I want to keep my job."

I gripped my skull and tried to think.

"I'll just sneak out after she goes to sleep."

"I guess we can do that." But I wouldn't be getting laid again. I'd have to wait until tomorrow.

She grabbed half of my sandwich and sat on the bed. She took small bites while she ate quietly. She didn't get crumbs everywhere like I did. Like Rae, she ate with grace that was borderline pretentious.

I sat beside her and ate my half.

"I hope everything is okay between them."

"I'm sure it's fine. They don't make any sense, but somehow, they make it work."

"I've warmed up to Ryker over the past few months." She finished her sandwich then wiped her hands on her jeans. "He was so standoffish before, but it seems like he really cares about her now."

"Yeah…" I still saw the horrifying ending. It was only a matter of time before Ryker did what he always did and took off. He claimed everything was different with Rae, but I didn't buy that. Their relationship had an expiration date, and I wished Rae would remember that.

***

"You're sure she's asleep?"

I cracked the door open and peered down the hallway to Rae's bedroom. The crack under the door was black so she was probably out for the night. Safari's feet weren't tapping against the hardwood floor like he was pacing, and I thought I heard his gentle snores. "Yeah. She's probably been asleep for a few hours."

"Okay. Let's be quiet."

We walked out the door then tiptoed down the hallway, doing our best to remain absolutely silent. The floorboard creaked underneath my foot, and I heard Safari's collar jiggle when he moved his head.

Damn dog.

We kept walking down the hallway and just reached the kitchen when I heard Rae's door open.

Motherfucker.

I pushed Kayden into the living room then blocked the end of the hallway with my size so Rae wouldn't step out and see Kayden standing there.

Rae walked out with her hair in a messy bun. She wore plaid pajama bottoms and a shirt too many sizes too big. She dragged her hand down her face in sleepiness then searched for the bathroom.

Then she spotted me. Her eyes squinted as she took me in. "What the hell are you doing?"

"Me? What the hell are you doing?"

"I've got to pee."

"Then pee."

She continued to narrow her eyes at me. "Why are you still standing there?"

"Because..."

"Because why? Go to bed."

"I'm..." I tried to think of an excuse so she wouldn't come sniffing around. Rae wasn't just smart, but observant. She would figure out I was trying to hide something and she would snoop—like always. "I'm watching porn in the living room. Didn't want you to see anything."

She made a face of pure disgust. "Oh my god, Rex. You're so damn gross. Didn't you just have a woman over here?"

"Yeah, but she wasn't very good in the sack."

"Pig." She finally walked into the bathroom. She slammed the door shut, and the toilet seat tapped when she opened the lid.

"Quick." I nodded for Kayden to come with me to the front door. I undid the locks and finally got it open. "Can you get home by yourself?"

"I'll be fine." She darted out.

"Wait." I went after her and gave her a quick kiss on the lips. "Text me when you get home."

Despite the urgency she had a moment ago, she smiled. "Okay."

I stared at her beautiful blue eyes and got lost for a moment, thinking about how bright they looked when I was thrusting into her from above. Her soft strands grazed across my fingertips, and I'd never touched hair so soft or that smelled so good. "Night."

"Night."

I shut the door just as Rae came out of the bathroom.

She stomped down the hallway, half asleep and ready to get back to bed. She didn't bother looking at me this time and didn't ask why I was standing in the doorway. She shut the door behind her and turned off her bedroom light.

I leaned against the counter and dragged my hands down my face, knowing that was a close call. Fooling around over here wasn't the best idea. In fact, it was flat-out stupid. Maybe I would need to move out even if that meant I wouldn't save as much money. I could have Kayden over whenever I wanted, and I could fuck her on every piece of furniture I possessed.

My cock got hard again.

Now I wished she wasn't gone.

Chapter Ten

Rex

I yawned so long my eyes watered.

Zeke watched me while he finished eating his chicken wing. He licked the sauce off his fingers and grabbed another.

I drank my beer then grabbed another wing from the pile. Before I took a bite, I yawned and popped my ears. My body was exhausted, and I was so tired I could barely think straight. After Kayden left, I couldn't get to bed right away because I was horny. I wanted to jerk off but I wanted to fuck her instead. Going from real pussy to my hand was such a step down.

Zeke watched me with a raised eyebrow.

This time, I tried not to yawn by keeping my mouth closed, but it happened again anyway. My eyes watered, and I took a bite of the atomic wing in my hand.

"Why are you so tired?" Zeke sipped his beer. "You've yawned five times in the past two minutes."

"I was up late last night."

"Playing Call of Duty?"

"No..." I wanted to come out and tell Zeke the truth, but I agreed with Kayden. Telling anyone was a stupid idea. Zeke would convince me to walk away before things got ugly, and he would probably tell Rae what was going on. If we kept it between us, we could do everything we wanted and then walk away from one another. No one would even know we hooked up and we could go back to being the friends we used to be. But it was still strange keeping the truth from him. "I had this chick over last night."

"That makes more sense." He finished his wing before he wiped his fingers on his napkin. "Pretty wild?"

I remembered the way she bounced on my dick like she needed my cock more than I needed her pussy. "I wouldn't say wild. But it was definitely amazing."

"Who's this chick?"

Now I had to outright lie, and I didn't feel good about it. "I met her a while ago when I was out. We became friends, and then she asked me if I could show her a few moves...because she's self-conscious about her performance."

"Then you must have taught her well," he said with a chuckle.

"That's the thing...she's perfect. She's an amazing kisser, she gives head like she's a professional, and she was awesome in the sack. She wants me to teach her how to be sexy, but she doesn't need my help. Honestly, I've learned some stuff from her."

"That's a pretty awesome arrangement."

"It almost seems too good to be true."

"When something good comes into your life, don't question it."

That was what I was doing. "I asked her about it and said I didn't want to ruin our friendship, but she said everything will be fine. So...I guess we have a booty call situation going on."

"Wait, how good of friends are you with this girl?"

I shrugged. "We're kinda close, I guess."

"Have I met her?"

"No..." Zeke was smart, and I hoped he didn't figure out who the real culprit was.

"What's her name?"

"Uh...Denise." It was the only thing I could think of off the top of my head. "We've seen each other around a lot, and sometimes I would see her when I played ball with Tobias. I wouldn't say we're super close, but we know each other pretty well." I started to sweat, so I wiped my forehead with the back of my forearm.

"Hot wings are pretty hot, huh?"

"What?" Now I perspired even more.

"The atomic sauce...it's really hot."

I finally pieced it together. "Yeah, I guess I'm not used to it." I took a long drink of my cold beer to cool off.

"So it's a friends with benefits type of situation?"

"Yeah, seems that way."

"Well, if you weren't really close, then I guess there's no harm in it. But I think something like that with Jessie or Kayden would be disastrous."

I held my breath until my chest ached with desperation. "I'm not sleeping with them."

"I know," he said. "I just meant—"

"Especially not Kayden. She and I don't click at all. I even told you how tense it is between us all the time. I don't like her hair, and she's got weird arms…not my type. Gross."

Zeke's expression hardened into one of suspicion. "You told me you thought both Jessie and Kayden were hot."

"I was just saying that to be nice. They're disgusting."

"That's a little harsh…"

"I'm not sleeping with either one of them, alright? Just want to get my point across." Why the hell was it so hot in there?

"Got it." He placed more wings on his plate and finally broke eye contact with me. The tension rose between us, and we ate in silence for several minutes.

I should have played that differently. I made myself look like a huge asshole. "Don't tell them I said that…"

"That you think Jess and Kayden are disgusting?" he asked sarcastically. "Yeah, I'm not going to go out of my way to make them cry."

"I'm not saying they're ugly. I'm just not attracted to them. That's all."

"Whatever, man." He picked at his fries.

At least it was better for him to think I was an ass than sleeping with Kayden. It was the lesser of two evils. "So…how are things with Rochelle?"

He perked up at the mention of her. "Great. We went hiking with her parents the other day."

"Whoa, hold on." I dropped my wing and leaned over the table. Zeke hadn't met a girlfriend's parents since we were in high school. I knew he was into her, but I didn't realize how serious this was. They'd only been dating for a month and they were moving at lightning speed. "You already met her folks?"

"Yeah, they're really nice. I like them."

"But…you don't think that's too soon?"

"Rochelle invited me to go along, and I didn't see the harm in it. Her dad is a heart surgeon so we had a lot to talk about."

I still thought that was crazy, and I was concerned he didn't think the same thing.

"We hiked Mount Rainier and then had lunch afterward. Her dad is an outdoor kind of guy, so he and I clicked pretty well. Her mother is really nice too. Rochelle looks a lot like her. And I'm pretty sure they liked me too."

Of course they did. Zeke was perfect. "That's cool..."

"I'm going over there for dinner on Friday. They live just outside of Seattle."

They already sounded like a married couple. "This sounds serious." Zeke was a grown man and could do whatever he wanted, but I was worried this was moving too fast and he wasn't thinking straight. Deep down inside, I thought Rochelle was just some kind of a rebound off Rae. When Rae got serious with Ryker, not only did Zeke realize he missed his chance, but he was probably never going to get a chance ever again. He wanted to move on and settle down as quickly as possible.

But should I tell him that?

Would it just piss him off?

Maybe meeting her parents wasn't that big of a deal and I was just reading too much into it. Rochelle really was an awesome girl so maybe his feelings were genuine. It wasn't like they were getting married or something.

Zeke finished chewing his bite before he answered. "Yeah, it feels serious. But I think that's a good thing."

He'd never been serious with anyone up until this point. I still thought it was strange that the one time he gets intense with someone is when Rae is in a committed relationship. I couldn't forget what he said about Rae to me, that he could see himself settling down with her. All of this couldn't have just been a coincidence. Right?

But I needed to just let it go. He knew more about his relationship than I did. I needed to butt out and mind my own business.

"Maybe the four of us can go on a double date."

I almost laughed because it was absurd. "Yeah, maybe."

***

"Take that, asshole." My fingers worked the controller, and I drove Zeke off the road.

"Son of a bitch." He made a serious comeback and slammed back into me, making me spin out and drive off the side of the road and into a tree. "Now look at who's an asshole."

I reversed the car and tried to get back on the road as quickly as possible.

Then the doorbell rang.

Zeke immediately hit pause. "That must be Rochelle."

"She's coming over?" I thought it would just be the two of us tonight.

"Yeah. I invited the rest of the gang, but Rae was busy with Ryker and Jessie has a date. So I think Kayden is coming." He walked away and headed to the door.

Kayden was coming over?

This had to be a joke.

Just her?

Automatically, my dick got hard.

Goddammit.

"Hey, baby." Zeke wrapped his arms around Rochelle's waist and kissed her on the mouth longer than necessary.

I looked back at the screen so I wouldn't throw up.

"I brought some chocolate covered popcorn." She handed him a Zip-Lock bag. "Made it myself."

"Thanks, baby." He kissed her again and set it on the counter. "Rex is in the living room."

Rochelle walked inside and gave me her typical sweet smile. She wore a pink dress with a belt around her waist. It was tight on her arms and her neck. She wore brown boots that went up to her knees. "Hey, Rex."

I used to really like Rochelle, but now that they were moving so fast, it made me wonder if she was taking advantage of him. She probably saw him as

Prince Charming, the biggest catch in the world, and I was afraid she was reeling him in too quickly.

But I had to remind myself it shouldn't matter.

"Hey. How's it going?" I stood up and hugged her. "Chocolate popcorn, huh?"

"My grandma taught me how to make it. It's actually really good. The popcorn is still crunchy even though the chocolate melted over it."

"I'll definitely give it a try. I inhale anything that's edible."

She laughed. "No wonder you and Zeke are best friends."

Zeke came into the living room and set the bowl of popcorn on the table. "It's pretty damn good."

I took a handful, and I was annoyed that it really was amazing. "This is awesome. If Rae were here, she'd hit that whole thing by herself."

"Thank god she's not," Zeke said with a laugh.

The doorbell rang again.

"That must be Kayden," Zeke said. "Can you get that?"

"Why do I have to get it?" My defensiveness lashed out immediately, and I couldn't control myself from snapping.

Zeke and Rochelle both stared at me like I was a bomb about to explode.

"It's cool..." Rochelle smiled through the tension. "I'll get it." She walked away and answered the door.

Zeke watched me with concern. "You alright, man?"

"Dude, I'm so good." I grabbed another handful of popcorn. "I just don't want to leave this stuff. I'm gonna hog it."

Zeke accepted the explanation and walked back into the kitchen. "Hey, Kayden."

"Hey." She was dressed in dark jeans with a black cardigan. It fit her petite frame perfectly and highlighted her hourglass figure. "I brought some wine." She held up the bottle. "You can never have too much booze, right?"

"Absolutely not." Zeke took it from her hands. "Thanks for this."

"No problem." Kayden glanced in my direction then quickly looked away.

I pretended she didn't exist.

"You look so cute," Rochelle said. "How do you stay so thin? Do you work out every day?"

"Oh, thanks," Kayden said modestly. "I spend so much time reading that I forget to eat sometimes."

And she gets a serious workout fucking me.

"Then I need to start reading more," Rochelle said with a laugh.

Zeke rolled his eyes. "Whatever, baby."

Kayden finally walked into the living room and headed right toward me. She wore a smile that was so cute I wanted to kiss her. "Hey, Rex."

"Hey." I kept the table between us and refused to let her get any closer. "Popcorn?" I held up the bowl.

"Oh cool." She grabbed a handful. "It's covered in chocolate."

"Rochelle made it." I sat on the other couch, trying to stay away from her. "Where's Jessie?" Things would be so much less awkward if there was another person there. Now it seemed like a double date. It made me paranoid that Zeke knew exactly what was going on. But that couldn't be right.

"She had a date." She continued to stand there and snack on the popcorn. Her eyes trailed to the TV. "Playing a game?"

"Racing game." I rested my ankle on the opposite knee out of nervousness, and then returned my foot to the floor. Since I couldn't sit still, I started to shake my knee. I rubbed the back of my neck just so I had something to do. Maybe I should lie and say I was sick so I could leave. I couldn't be in the same room with

Kayden like this and act normal. I wasn't even sure what normal was.

Zeke and Rochelle came back into the living room and sat on the other couch. Zeke's arm immediately went around Rochelle's shoulders. "You guys wanna watch a movie? Rochelle hasn't seen Star Wars, and I've been meaning to show it to her."

"Hasn't seen Star Wars?" I blurted. "Are you serious?"

Rochelle shrugged. "We didn't have a TV when I was growing up."

Wasn't her father a surgeon? "Oh…"

"And we were always so busy as kids we didn't have time to watch movies and stuff."

What a freak. "Oh…" It was all I could think of to say. How could Zeke be this serious with a woman who had never seen Star Wars? It was one of our favorite movies of all time. "You need to watch it. Like, yesterday."

"Then let's do it." Zeke grabbed the remote and hit a few buttons. When the TV didn't respond, he eyed Kayden. "Sorry, you're blocking the signal. Why don't you take a seat?"

She stared at the seat beside me before she approached.

I immediately scooted to the opposite end of the couch so we were nowhere near each other. I didn't even want to smell her.

She sat at the opposite end and crossed her legs. Her gaze was focused on the TV.

"Does she annoy you?" Rochelle asked with a laugh.

"Huh?" I blurted.

"You guys are sitting so far apart," she noted. "It just looks funny."

"I just farted." It was all I could think of, and after I said it, I realized I could have made up a much better excuse.

Kayden immediately cringed even though it wasn't true.

"Good thing we're on this couch, baby." Zeke leaned in and kissed her. "I've been the victim of those farts. Trust me, they're terrible."

"Like yours aren't," I said defensively.

"Let's face it," Rochelle said. "All farts are bad. There's no contest."

"I don't know," Kayden said. "Rex's are pretty bad. It's all that bowling alley food he eats."

I turned my defensiveness on her. "Whoa, I've never farted around you."

"Yes, you have," Kayden said. "Loads of times."

"Well, not since—" I stopped myself from saying something really stupid. "It's been a while…"

Zeke finally got the movie going and the theme music started. "Here we go. Baby, prepare to be amazed."

She cupped his face and kissed him hard on the mouth. "I already am amazed."

***

"Are you sure you don't want to stay?" Zeke asked Rochelle at the door.

"I've got to get up early tomorrow for that meeting." She cupped his cheeks and kissed him. "But I'll stay over tomorrow."

"Alright," he said sadly.

"Love you."

What the fuck?

"Love you too." He gave her another quick peck before he watched her walk to her car.

They were saying the L word? Zeke had never told a woman he loved her and he was thirty.

Could this really be happening?

"I'm going to go too." Kayden gave him a hug. "I'll see you around."

Zeke hugged her back before he let her go.

Kayden gave me a look full of meaning before she walked to her car.

I knew exactly what that meant. "I'm gonna go too. You know, gotta take out Safari..." Was I making it obvious?

"Alright." He clapped my shoulder. "See you around. Keep those farts in check."

"Huh? What?" I was busy thinking about how I was going to fuck Kayden.

"You know...because you farted earlier." Zeke stared into my eyes like he was looking for something. "Everything alright? You seem distracted."

"Dude, I'm good," I said quickly. "Just tired. See you later." I walked out before he could say anything more. If he asked too many questions, he might get an answer I wasn't ready to give.

***

The sex was good, like I expected. We screwed on her bed, her on all fours. I stared at her gorgeous ass and her puckered little asshole as I rammed into her from behind. I got a hold of her neck and slammed into her until my cock sang with release.

We lay side by side, both covered in sweat and out of breath.

I blurted out the first thing that came to my mind. "Did you hear Zeke tell Rochelle he loved her?"

She ran her fingers through her hair and her chest continued to rise and fall from exhaustion. "Yeah. So?"

"You don't think it's too soon?"

She turned her head my way. "The first thing you think of after sex is your best friend?"

"No…I thought about other stuff before that." I kept my eyes glued to the ceiling.

"Like?"

"How good you are in bed." That was the truth. I had a quick replay in my head of all the highlights. I was particularly fascinated by the sight of her tight asshole. I wanted to stick my fingers inside, but I thought it was too soon in our arrangement for that.

"Well, I guess that makes it better…"

"So you don't think it's weird they've already said the L word?"

She shrugged. "I don't know. I guess I don't really care."

"It's just…Zeke's never moved this fast before."

She propped herself up on her elbow and looked down at me, her tits pressed into my arm and her hair touching my neck. "Do you not like Rochelle?"

"No, I think she's great. I've liked her from the beginning."

"Then what's the problem?"

I couldn't tell her my theory about Rae because she would tell her the second she had the chance. "I'm just concerned he's rushing into it for the wrong reasons. And he'll hurt her and himself in the process."

"What wrong reasons?"

I shrugged. "I don't know…just in general."

"I think you're reading too much into it. Rochelle is really nice, she's a doctor too, and she clearly makes him happy. That's all that matters."

"Yeah…I guess you're right."

"Unless there's something you aren't telling me?" She drilled her gaze into my eyes like she could read my mind. Her hand glided up and down my chest with affection, and she nearly coaxed the truth right out of me.

"No." I turned my gaze back to the ceiling and changed the subject. "So did you like the movie?"

Ray of Hope

Chapter Eleven

Rae

I sat at the kitchen table and ate my Fruity Pebbles with Safari lying at my feet. His eyes constantly watched every movement in the hope something tasty would fall onto the floor and turn into a snack.

Rex walked in wearing sweatpants and a t-shirt. His hair was a disaster, and he was so sleepy he nearly knocked over the coffee pot when he tried to grab it. "Damn kitchen…" He finally got his grip on the handle and poured himself a mug. Of course, he spilled it across the counter and didn't even notice.

Whatever.

He finally made it to the table and fell into the chair opposite me. He rested his face against his hand and stared into his mug with one eye closed. It seemed like he might fall asleep just sitting there. Then he finally took a drink and cringed. "Man, this tastes like shit…"

"It wouldn't if you cleaned out the coffee pot like I asked."

"If you're so obsessed with this place being sterile, maybe you should hire a maid."

"And maybe you should—" I stopped myself from escalating the argument. "It's too early on a Saturday for this. Forget it."

"Sounds good to me." He eyed my bowl of cereal across the table. "Any left?"

"Tons."

"Sweet. But I'm too tired to get up."

"Why didn't you just keep sleeping?"

He rubbed his temple. "Migraine."

"Crazy night at Zeke's?" I thought they were hanging out to watch a movie, but maybe it turned into a game over a round of shots. It wouldn't be the first time.

"Kinda."

"When did you get home?"

"Pretty late."

I didn't hear him walk in so it must have been really early in the morning.

"Have fun with Ryker?"

"Yeah. It was good." I returned to eating my cereal, falling into comfortable silence with Rex.

He stared into his coffee again, looking ill. "What do you think of Rochelle?"

It was a random ass question. "Zeke's girlfriend?"

"Yeah."

"What kind of question is that?"

"What do you think of her?" he repeated. "I thought you were smart enough to understand English with that fancy degree of yours."

I ignored the jab because dishes were about to fly across the room. "I think she's great. But since you're asking, I can only assume you don't care for her."

"I really liked her when I first met her, but now I don't know."

"What did she do?" I hadn't met one of Zeke's girlfriends that I didn't like. They were always down to earth, friendly, and cool to hang out with. Rochelle didn't seem any different. She always wore a smile on her face, and she looked at Zeke like he was the greatest thing that ever happened to her.

"Zeke told me he met her parents, and they're saying the L word to each other."

Their relationship moved quickly, faster than any relationship I'd seen him in. Girls came and went, but after a few months, they usually disappeared. Zeke lost interest and wanted to be single again. He didn't talk about it much. "Then maybe she's the one."

"But he doesn't even know her."

I shrugged. "He knows her better than we do."

"I think he's lost his mind."

Rex never said anything mean about anyone, besides me. It was out of character for him to be so negative toward Rochelle. "What's the big deal? Are you afraid your best friend is going to settle down and forget about you?" Is that what it boiled down to? "Because he's your best friend, you should be happy for him."

"Look, I'm looking out for her too. She's just a rebound, and she's going to get shattered."

"A rebound from what?" Maybe Zeke had serious feelings for someone but it didn't work out. And he never mentioned it to any of us.

Rex quickly stared down into his coffee. "Some girl he was talking to a while ago. He was into her but she was kind of a flake."

I'm surprised he never told me that. "Either way, I think you should just let it go. Zeke is a man, and he can make his own decisions. If he loves her, so do we. End of story." No one trusted Ryker in the beginning, but they slowly warmed up to him, including Rex. We should all do the same for Rochelle.

"Yeah...whatever."

***

"Safari, chill." I tugged on the leash attached to his chest and tried to get him to slow down. I dug my feet into the concrete so I had the strength to hold him back. "I said we were going for a walk, not a sprint."

Ryker chuckled beside me, wearing his running shorts with a gray t-shirt. No matter what he wore, he looked sexy as hell. His five o'clock shadow was thick because he didn't bother shaving that morning. His eyes were bright despite the overcast sky. A gift from the heavens, Ryker was a treat for anyone with eyes. "He's just excited."

"Then you handle him." I handed over the leash.

He chuckled and held up his hand. "No, thanks. He's your dog."

"He might pull me along to some other hot guy." We walked forward, Safari still tugging a little too hard on his leash.

"Hope not. I'll have to kick his ass."

"For being hot?" I asked incredulously.

"No. So he won't be hot anymore." He nudged me in the side playfully. "I've got to eliminate the competition, you know."

"Ryker, there's no competition when it comes to you." I dropped our playful banter and turned serious when I didn't mean to. It slipped out, and I dropped my guard. Ryker turned me into mush and he knew it, so it wasn't that alarming.

"Yeah?" He gave me that sexy smile mixed with a smolder then came close to me. He leaned down and kissed me as we walked, the hair from his jaw rubbing against my skin in a tantalizing way.

Anytime I felt it, I pictured his face between my legs and that beard prickling my skin. "Yeah."

He pulled away, still looking smug. "Say things like that more often."

"So your ego will get bigger?"

"No. So I'll know you're hooked on me."

I released a sarcastic snort. "You already knew that."

"A little positive reinforcement never hurt anyone."

Safari dragged me along even harder, pulling me through the park and past another jogger. "Goddammit, Safari." I dug my feet into the concrete again. "Why do you always act like a brat when Ryker is around?"

"Maybe he wants to give us some privacy."

"No." I yanked on the leash. "He just wants to sniff someone's ass."

Ryker laughed from behind me, watching me try to tame my dog.

He kept pulling me along until we stopped right in front of some guy. Safari immediately sniffed his crotch.

"Do you have any manners?" I pulled Safari away so his nose wasn't buried in this man's shorts. "I'm so sorry. He's just—" I looked up and saw Matt staring at me, his eyes looking displeased with Ryker beside me. "Oh. Hey, Matt." I tried to recover from the shock of seeing the last terrible date I had before I found Ryker. I would never forget the way he shoved his tongue up my nose during our good night kiss. It was the last bad date before Ryker blew me away with his incredible—and less sloppy—moves. I tried to appear as normal as possible, but the tension was getting to me.

He stared at me with a look I'd never seen before. It was like he hated me. "Texted you a few times and never got a response. Glad to see you're alright." The anger in his voice contradicted all the concern he just showed me.

"Well, you know…" I didn't want to come out and say I didn't want to see him again. He didn't know Ryker, but I didn't want to embarrass him in front of another guy. "How's the firehouse?"

His eyes darted to Ryker and his anger burned brighter. "Looks like you moved on to a new boy toy."

It's not like Matt was my boy toy prior to Ryker. "Well, it was nice seeing you. Take care." I pulled Safari away so we could remove ourselves from the most awkward conversation ever.

"I'm sure I'll see you around town picking up every guy you see." He turned away, his shoulder tense in his firefighter t-shirt.

I ignored the jab because it wasn't worth my time. I walked with Safari. "Glad that's over…" I turned to Ryker but realized he wasn't there.

Oh no…

"Allow me to introduce myself." Ryker stepped in front of Matt but didn't extend his hand. "I'm Ryker, Rae's boyfriend." He got dangerously close to him, towering over Matt with his height and strength. Even though Matt was a firefighter, he seemed small in comparison to Ryker. "And you're going to apologize for that asshole comment."

Matt stood his ground but didn't speak.

Ryker took a step forward. "Get to it."

"Ryker, it's fine…" I didn't want this to explode into an unnecessary fight. People were already staring at the commotion with their phones held up in the hope of something to record.

Ryker took another step forward, making Matt step back. "You insult my girl, you insult me. It's not her fault you're a terrible date and an even worse kisser. Man up and admit the girl just didn't like you. She wasn't interested, which is completely her right. But that doesn't give you the right to imply she's a whore. Now apologize."

I held my breath as I waited for someone to throw a punch. I thought Matt might, but if he had dishonorable conduct, he could be punished at the fire house. He loved his job and couldn't afford to lose it. Ryker had a lot on the line too, an entire company he represented. But I had a feeling he didn't care.

Matt stepped back and turned around. When he looked at me, he didn't wear the same look of pure hatred. Now he seemed indifferent, like he wanted to get away from Ryker and me as quickly as possible. "Sorry."

"That was a shitty apology and you know it," Ryker barked.

Matt sighed before he spoke. "I'm sorry for what I said."

"Much better," Ryker said. "Now you can go."

Matt turned on his heel and immediately walked away. He moved as fast as he could without running. Everyone watched him disappear before they finally returned to their routines. People put their phones away when they realized there wouldn't be a brawl.

"You didn't have to do that." I didn't need a man to fight my battles. I would have defended myself if I cared enough to. I knew Matt was just hurt deep down inside, that he wanted us to turn into something more than a simple date. He didn't handle it very well, and I wasn't justifying him basically calling me a whore, but I understood his hatred stemmed from pain. Seeing me with a new man who was obviously attractive just made him more jealous.

"Yes, I did." Ryker came to my side and wrapped his arm around my waist. "Every decent man in the world would have done the same thing. It's not okay for him to talk to you that way. It's not okay for him to call you a whore just because you wouldn't sleep with him. It's not okay to be a dick just because he didn't get what he wanted." He hugged me hard against him and looked me in the eye. "Especially when it comes to my woman."

***

"So relaxing." I lay against the wall of the tub with my head resting on the towel.

Ryker was on the opposite side of the enormous hot tub, his chest looking appetizing as beads of water dripped down the grooves of his abdominal muscles. "Really?" He cocked his head to the side, his jaw stern and his eyes indifferent.

"You're not?"

"Not really. You're sitting in a tub of warm water as it slowly cools to room temperature."

When we came home from our jog, we got nasty on his bed. We skipped dinner because neither one of us were hungry. But afterward, I wanted to slip into his tub. I'd seen it in his master bathroom but it was never used. "Then why do you have one?"

"It came with the place."

"And you've never used it?"

He shook his head. "I'm not even in the shower this long."

"Not even when you beat off?"

He immediately grinned when I said anything sexual. "I don't like to stand when I jerk off. I prefer to sit."

"Lazy?"

"Nah. I just like to watch porn as I do it. Can't bring my laptop in here."

"You don't use your imagination?" I liked to let my mind wander when I had a go with my vibrator.

"Not really."

"Even now, you still do it that way?" He didn't picture me when he went to town on himself?

"Do what what way?"

"Jerk off to porn."

"I haven't jerked off since you came into the picture."

I laughed because it was absurd. "I'm not that kind of woman. I really don't care."

He raised an eyebrow. "You think I'm lying?"

"Definitely."

"I'm really telling you the truth." He rested his arms along the curve of the tub, the water and bubbles draining down.

"Cut the shit," I said with a laugh. "It's me."

Now his eyes narrowed. "If I did, I would admit it. But I don't. I've never been in a long-term relationship before so I didn't know what to expect. But honestly, I don't have the urge. But now I'm concerned…"

"About?"

"Do you touch yourself when I'm not around?"

I grinned from ear to ear. "This conversation isn't about me. It's about you."

"Nope. You aren't getting out of this after you interrogated me like that." His hands disappeared under the water and he grabbed my thigh. "Now answer me."

"What does it matter?"

He gave me a gentle squeeze. "It matters to me."

"Sometimes..." I looked away and sipped my glass of wine.

He didn't seem aroused by that confession. In fact, he seemed annoyed. "Am I not doing a good job?"

"You are. Actually, you're doing a really good job. That's the problem."

He looked at me like he didn't understand.

"I'm charged a lot. I spend a few days with you, come home, and then I remember everything. Then I need more..."

Now Ryker just looked annoyed. "I never thought I would say this, but I'm a little jealous."

"Jealous?" I asked with a laugh.

"I don't want you to touch yourself anymore."

"That's a weird request. It's not like I don't think about you."

"I still feel like I'm not doing my job right."

"You are. Honestly, it's not an insult to your performance."

"Well, I'm taking it that way." He looked out the window and to the city beyond. "Whenever you need a fix, I want you to call me."

"You can't be serious." Sometimes it happened late at night or early in the morning before work.

"Dead. Serious."

"It lasts five minutes and then it's over. It's usually a quickie before I go to work or something."

"Don't care. Call me, and I'll be there."

"You're going to come all the way to my apartment just to fuck me then leave?" That sounded like a lot of extra time and work.

"Yes."

"Every time I tell you I'm horny?"

"Yes."

"I don't think you understand just how horny I am."

He didn't crack a smile. "I want you to call me the second goose bumps form on your arm. End of story."

If he was serious, I wasn't going to complain. I had a sexy man at my beck and call the second I snapped my fingers. Everything worked out in my favor. "Sounds good to me."

"Good. The only fingers that should be down there are mine."

"Alright." I sipped my wine again. "But there really is nothing to be jealous of. You're the only man I think about."

"Not good enough. I don't want you to think about me. I want you to be with me."

A little intense, but that was okay. It sounded like more orgasms were on the way.

"We have an understanding?"

I nodded. "Looks like we do."

***

Zeke raised his hand in the crowd so I could see him. "Over here."

When I spotted him, I joined him to the side. We decided to meet at Pike's Market for lunch. We invited Rex, but he was too busy at Groovy Bowl to leave. "Hey. I'm sorry I'm late."

"It's fine. I don't have an appointment for another hour anyway so we're good." He smiled then walked beside me as we went into the deli. "What are you getting? The BBQ beef?"

I always got the same thing whenever we went there. "Yeah…it's so good."

"Then let's get extra napkins," he teased. "You always make a mess of yourself."

"It's really messy, alright?"

"Then why do you always order it?" he asked with a laugh.

"I'm telling you, it's delicious."

We ordered our food then got a seat by the window. It was drizzling outside, but we were both used to the constant rainfall. I took my waterproof jacket everywhere I went, and today, I didn't bother doing my hair since it was going to turn into wet mush anyway.

I unrolled my sandwich and went to town.

Zeke stared at me with a partially hidden grin. He ate his turkey sandwich and chips, careful not to get it on his collared shirt and tie. He looked too young to be a doctor, like he skipped several grades. "How's work?"

"Alright. Jenny called in sick so I'm in the lab alone."

"Better than being stuck in a lab with a sick person."

"I get lonely sometimes. Wish I could take Safari with me to work."

"Ryker doesn't stop by?"

"Once in a blue moon," I said. "He's usually busy upstairs, and we don't want to make it obvious we're seeing each other."

"I can see the hazards." He grabbed a handful of chips and dropped them into his mouth.

"So you'll never guess who I ran into at the park the other day." I wiped the BBQ sauce off my fingertips then rested my elbows on the table.

He pointed to the corner of his mouth. "You got sauce everywhere."

I quickly wiped it away without breaking my stride. "Remember that firefighter I went out with? You know, the one who stuck his tongue up my nose."

Zeke laughed at the memory. "Like I could forget."

"Ryker and I were jogging when we ran into him."

He finished his bag of chips before he crinkled it into a ball. "Was that awkward?"

"Very. Matt was pretty annoyed to see me with some other guy."

"Why?" His humor immediately dropped. "You haven't seen him in months."

"But he was really infatuated with me and was pretty upset when I never called him back."

Zeke shook his head. "It's just how it goes sometimes. No need to get angry."

"He made a few mean comments then straight up called me a whore."

Now Zeke was just pissed. "Are you fucking serious?"

"Ryker got angry and forced him to apologize. Then he walked away."

"Good. If he didn't, I would have taken care of it."

"I didn't tell you the story to make you upset." I spoke in a calm voice so he would mellow out. "I just thought it was ironic. I mean, if Matt really wanted to get a girlfriend, he could try kissing her mouth instead of her nose."

Zeke didn't laugh but his anger was definitely dimming. "I'm glad Ryker stood up for you. He's a good guy."

"I didn't need him to."

"He has no right to call you his girlfriend unless he bends over backward for you. If it were Rochelle, Matt would be knocked out cold on the pavement. I wouldn't put up with that shit."

This was a new side to Zeke I wasn't used to. He was always loyal and protective, but not full of rage like this. "If anything happened, Safari would have taken him out. So Ryker didn't need to do anything."

"True," he said. "Safari would have bitten his face off at your command."

"But Matt didn't deserve that, despite what he said."

Zeke rolled his eyes. "That guy is such a loser. What was Jessie thinking when she set you up with him?"

I shrugged. "I don't know. I'm sure he made a better impression with her. He is cute, so she wasn't wrong about that. But everything else about him sucks."

"You're too good for him in either case."

I smiled. "Thanks..."

"I think you're too good for Ryker too. But then again, I think that about every guy."

"Then who can I date?" I asked with a laugh.

He sipped his soda for ten seconds before he finally looked at me again. "Good point."

I ate the first half of my sandwich and got it all over my hands and my mouth. I could feel the sauce caking in the corners and just below my nose.

Thankfully, I asked for more napkins because I wouldn't know where to start.

Zeke stared at me, clearly debating whether he should bother telling me about the shit all over my face.

"I'm just going to wait until I'm done."

"It'll save you some napkins," he said with a chuckle.

"So things seem serious with Rochelle."

He averted his gaze and stared at the table while he ate. "Sorry, I can't take you seriously when you look like that."

"Whatever," I said as I rolled my eyes. "I look the same."

"I beg to differ." He took a few bites of his sandwich before he spoke. "Yeah, things have been great with her. But why do you think things are serious?"

"Rex said you guys are using the L word."

"Oh...I didn't know he heard that." His voice trailed away.

"What does it matter if he did or didn't?"

He shrugged. "Just a weird thing to say in front of a friend."

"I don't think it's weird. If you love her, you love her. So it is serious then?"

He came out of his awkwardness once I showed him there was nothing to be concerned about. "Yeah, we are. Kinda just happened."

"Good for you. I thought she might be the one when I found out she was a doctor."

He shook his head. "I don't care about that. I mean, we have a lot in common but her career wasn't the most important thing to me."

"Then what was important?"

He took a moment to compose an answer. "She really makes an effort to be part of our group. I told her how important you guys are to me, and she respects that. She's sweet and kind...she makes me laugh. I mean, she's just great to be around."

"I'm happy for you." I finished my sandwich and wiped my mouth with a napkin. "She does seem like a terrific girl."

"She is." He finished his sandwich then rolled up the paper it was wrapped in. "What about you and Ryker? It's been a few months now."

"I know...time goes by fast." And so does the sex.

"Honestly, I didn't think it was going to last this long. But I'm glad I was wrong." When Zeke looked at me, there was sincerity in his eyes. Both he and Rex weren't big fans of our relationship but they butted out like friends were supposed to do. "Ryker must think you're the one."

"The one?"

"Yeah. I've never seen him with a girlfriend before. I've never seen him with the same girl for more than a day, actually. And with the amount of time that's passed…I could only assume he's head over heels."

"I wish." I wished he was just as obsessed with me as I was with him. I knew he enjoyed being around me and didn't want to be with anyone else, but I didn't think that affection went further than that.

"I'm serious, Rae. The guy is in love."

"No way." Sometimes I liked to pretend he was.

"Let me put it into perspective for you." He tossed his extra napkins onto my tray because he knew I would need them. "I know Rochelle and I have moved really fast, but it's obvious how I feel about her. Have you seen me with the same woman this long before? Have you seen me spend this much time with someone?"

"No…"

"And there's a reason for that. And Ryker is doing the exact same thing with you. Rae, you're a diamond in the rough. There aren't any women out there like you. Believe me, I've been around. You're beautiful, smart, and you play ball better than LeBron James." He chuckled before he continued. "Ryker isn't stupid. He knows a catch when he sees one. Maybe he hasn't said it, but there's no doubt he loves you."

My heart nearly stopped beating when I heard Zeke say that. A part of me believed him, and the other part wanted to believe him. "You really think so?"

He leaned over the table and lowered his voice. "I know so."

Ray of Hope

Chapter Twelve

Rae

I shut down the lab equipment and took off my lab coat before I scrubbed my hands in the sink. Not only did I wash my fingers, but under my nails, my knuckles, and even my arms up to the elbow. I didn't want to take any unwanted bacteria home so it could spread in my apartment, especially when Safari could be affected by it.

"Personally, I think you look hotter in a lab coat."

I smiled and pulled the paper towels out of the dispenser. "Even though it's ten sizes too big and covered in stains?"

"Especially."

I threw the towels in the garbage before I turned around. "Then you're into some weird shit." I saw him stand in a black suit and tie, looking beautiful like always.

"No, I'm just into you." He stood dangerously close to me but he didn't lean in for a kiss, knowing we were at work, and I would say no if he tried. "Big plans tonight?"

"Just with my vibrator."

His eyes immediately narrowed.

"Kidding. Geez, take a joke."

"I will when you say a good one."

"No, I don't have any plans tonight, other than cuddling with Safari. What about you?"

His eyes smoldered and he didn't even realize it. He possessed natural perks that made him innately sexy without any effort. "I wanted to take my woman out for dinner and dessert. And of course, some good sex afterward."

"Ooh...you've got my attention." I crossed my arms over my chest and tried not to be self-conscious about my messy bun and lack of makeup. Ryker almost never came down there so I didn't exactly doll myself up for the possibility.

"Is that a yes?"

"Ryker, it's always a yes."

"Great. Meet at my apartment at seven."

"Alright."

***

"Honey, I'll be back in the morning." I scratched him behind the ears and pouted my lips. "Rex will be here all night so you won't be alone."

Safari whined anyway.

"I love you too. But Mommy needs some alone time."

Rex grabbed a beer from the fridge. "Would you just go already? He doesn't understand a word you're saying."

"Yes, he does," I said defensively. "Dogs are smart."

"Not that smart." He turned to Safari. "No offense, man."

I gave my dog a kiss before I grabbed my clutch and walked to the door. "I'll see you tomorrow."

"Like, what time?" Rex never asked a question like that before.

"Whenever I come back. Why?"

He shrugged. "I may have a woman over or something. It would be nice to know if we have company."

I rolled my eyes. "Probably around noon."

"Thanks." He gave me a thumbs up before he walked away.

I finally walked out and headed to Ryker's.

***

The elevator doors opened, and Ryker was standing there waiting for me. He looked me up and down, eyeing my short olive dress and black heels. He whistled quietly, taking in my curled hair, exaggerated makeup, and the slutty clothes I wore. "Damn. You're going to get fucked good tonight."

"How romantic…" I wrapped my arms around his neck and kissed him slowly on the mouth.

His hands went to the small of my back and he hugged me hard, his fingertips moving to my ass for a squeeze. "You know that's how I'm romantic." He kissed the corner of my mouth before he rubbed his nose against mine. He continued to massage my ass like he wanted to stay at the apartment instead. "Where's your overnight bag?"

It dawned on me that I forgot it in my bedroom. I closed my eyes as the frustration washed over me. "Damn, I left it at home."

"No big deal. You can wear my stuff."

"I need my other things too."

"Like?"

I narrowed my eyes. "You're nosy."

"Just curious."

"My birth control, for one—"

"Let's pick it up before dinner." He gave me another kiss before he grabbed his keys and wallet.

"I'm not sure if I can look Safari in the eyes and say goodbye again…"

Ryker rolled his eyes. "He's just a dog. He'll get over it."

"I know. It's just hard sometimes. Rex pays attention to him but not the way I do."

"He'll be fine, sweetheart." He took my hand and walked me to the elevator and then the garage down below. "I do admire how affectionate you are with that dog...even if he gets in my path to you."

"Awe. You love him too. I can tell." I realized the error of my words but I just went with it. I opened the passenger door and got inside so he wouldn't see my face.

He got behind the wheel and shut the door behind him. He had no visible reaction on his face so it wasn't clear what he was thinking. "He is a pretty cool dog. After all, he was the one who introduced me to you." He started the engine then gave me that expression that contained a smile.

I smiled back. "True. He's our matchmaker."

***

I got the door unlocked and walked inside. "Rex, it's me—" I stopped in my tracks when I came face to face with Kayden. She stood in the kitchen, and she looked just as shocked to see me as I was to see her. Her hair was styled perfectly and she was dressed like she was about to go clubbing. She was just pouring two glasses of wine when she stopped. "Kayden?"

"Hey…" She set the bottle down and tucked her hair behind her ear. "Wow, you look cute. Where did you get that dress?"

"Target…when did you get here?" I was gone for fifteen minutes at the most.

Ryker came in behind me and looked at her with the same suspicion.

Rex's heavy feet came down the hallway. "Baby, do you know where—"

"Awe, where's Safari?" Kayden walked out of the kitchen and to the hallway. "I haven't seen him in so long. Your sister is looking for him."

"Who are you calling baby?" I blurted. "And I wasn't looking for Safari."

Rex entered the kitchen, looking wide eyed and terrified. "I thought you weren't going to be home until tomorrow?"

"I forgot my stuff," I snapped. "And what does it matter? What are the two of you doing?"

"Hanging out," Rex said. "What does it look like we're doing?"

"Just the two of you?" I put my hand on my hip and stared at the scene before me. There were two glasses of wine but Rex didn't even drink wine.

"No, not just the two of us," Kayden said quickly. "Jess is on the way, and Zeke and Rochelle are stopping by."

"Oh, really?" Now everything made sense. I had no idea why I jumped to any conclusion. I guess seeing Kayden there so quickly threw me off. "That sounds like fun. I forgot my bag in my room so I'm just going to grab it real quick."

"Hate it when that happens." Rex stepped off to the side so I could get past.

I grabbed my stuff, gave Safari another painful goodbye, and then returned to the front door. "I'm ready to go."

"Alright." Rex circled his arm around my waist. "You two have a fun night." He walked me out and shut the door behind us.

We got into the car then drove to the restaurant downtown. After we checked in at the front desk, we moved to our table against the window and ordered our drinks. I was starving so I got an appetizer. I needed something to munch on while we waited for our food.

"I still think Kayden is into Rex." The statement came out of nowhere. Sitting across the table with his expansive shoulders and unbelievably handsome face, Ryker could say anything and make it fit into the moment.

"What?" I just had a bite of calamari but I stopped to speak.

"It's so obvious. She's trying to spend as much time with him as she can. Not sure if Rex is aware of it."

He mentioned this at the arcade when we first started dating, but I didn't think anything of it. "I really doubt it. She said everyone was meeting over there so it's not like it's just the two of them for tonight."

He leaned back into his chair, that smug look in his eyes. "Text Jessie and ask her what she's doing tonight."

"Are you joking?"

"No. I'm serious."

"I'm not gonna do that." I ate more calamari.

"Why not?"

"Because it's stupid. If Kayden said that's what they're doing, then that's what they're doing. She wouldn't lie to me."

"She would if she was trying to protect herself..."

"I'm not gonna do it." I sipped my lemon drop and focused on the undeniably sexy man in front of me. "I'm not that kind of person and never will be."

Ryker dropped the subject but he still had a knowing look in his eyes.

The waiter finally brought dinner, and I nearly inhaled my food. I skipped lunch that afternoon because I had to pick up Jenny's slack since she was sick. Not eating all day made me grouchy and impatient.

Ryker ate his food slowly, cutting into each piece of his meat before placing it into his mouth with pure elegance. He chewed each bite slowly before he moved on to the next piece, not making a mess like I usually did. He sipped his wine and enjoyed it but he didn't make small talk with me.

I didn't make small talk with him either. I was a little annoyed he assumed my best friend would lie to me. And I was more annoyed that he wanted me to snoop around to figure out if she was taking me for a ride. I didn't assume my closest friends were liars, and I certainly didn't go out of my way to prove it.

"You look beautiful tonight."

"Thank you. But I know you're saying that because I'm mad."

"You're right," he whispered. "But I also mean it." He drank his wine before he pushed my glass closer to me. "Lighten up, sweetheart. I meant no offense."

"I know…I'm just touchy when it comes to stuff like that."

"Lying?"

"No. Questioning the loyalty of my friends. I don't have parents, grandparents, aunts and uncles…I only have them. And when someone insults them, I'm very offended by it."

He gave a slight nod. "I see. But I didn't insult them. I just think Kayden has feelings for Rex. That's all."

Maybe I was overreacting. I was extremely protective of my group of friends. It was hard for me to chill out about it sometimes. "You're right. I'm sorry."

"Apology accepted. But does this constitute as a fight?"

"I don't know. Why?"

"Because I wouldn't mind having some make up sex." His eyes smoldered as they burned into mine.

Anytime he gave me that look, I was a puddle on the ground. "I wouldn't either."

***

"Right here." He dropped his jeans and boxers to his ankles then sat in the center of the couch. A full length mirror was on the opposite wall and he could see his own reflection. He tapped his thigh then beckoned me into his lap.

I straddled his hips before I lowered myself on his thighs, his cock moving right between my ass cheeks.

Ryker leaned back against the couch and his eyes moved to the mirror. "Just like that…" He rocked his hips slightly and pushed his length through my crack.

As he watched us move together, his eyes darkened and his breathing made his powerful chest rise and fall at a fast pace.

"You want to stare at my ass while you fuck me?" I gripped his shoulders with my tits in front of his face. As I moved up and down, they shook slightly.

"Exactly." Both of his hands moved across my cheeks and gave them a tight squeeze. "I used to be a tit man before you came along. But now I'm both." He leaned forward and sucked my nipple into his mouth, swirling his tongue over the surface as his hot breath blanketed it with warmth.

My pussy clenched at the sight of the arousal in his eyes. Knowing I turned him on so much, that he squeezed me harder because he couldn't wait to be inside me, that he couldn't keep his breathing in control because he wanted to fuck me so hard, made my body immediately soaked with lubrication.

My hands dug into his bare shoulders, feeling the grooves between the muscles of his extraordinary strength. His cock continued to slide against me, and I waited for him to push inside me, to stretch me apart so wide I whimpered with both pleasure and pain.

Ryker watched my body in the mirror, staring at my ass on his lap and the deep curve of my back. I was contorting my body harder, making it bend so the small muscles surrounding my spine would protrude out. "Sexiest thing I've ever seen. I could do this all day if I didn't want to fuck you so bad." He lifted my ass with one hand then inserted the tip of cock with the other. He slowly stretched me, immediately reaching my slickness and pushing through it. He practically glided inside as he moved through my slippery channel. He gripped me by the hips and slowly lowered me until he was completely sheathed. "Fuck." The word came from deep in his throat, husky and loud.

He kept me in place on his cock, his entire nine inches deep inside me. He rocked my hips gently, moving them in a circular motion. His hand moved across my cheeks and gripped them both with his long fingers. "Your ass is unbelievable." His fingers grazed my crack and moved across my opening.

"I sit on it every day." I brushed my lips across his as I spoke.

He pulled my bottom lip into his mouth and gave me an aggressive kiss. Then he moved his fingers to my mouth and gently inserted them inside, getting them wet against my tongue. "Suck."

I sucked on his fingers and watched the fire burn in his eyes. He had manly hands, the kind that were veiny across the surface and full of detailed muscles that were prominent with every little move he made.

He pulled them out then returned them to my ass. His fingers found my back entry and slowly started to move inside.

"Whoa. I don't do ass play." Ryker was sexy as hell and could do almost anything to me, but my ass was not a playground.

"Have you tried?"

"No. And I intend to keep it that way."

He kept his fingers at my entryway but didn't push inside. "Do you trust me, sweetheart?" He kissed the corner of my mouth, making his voice dark and sexy. "When have I let you down?"

"Never."

"Then let me." He kissed me again, his warm breath falling on my face.

"Don't you think this is hot enough?"

"You're always hot, sweetheart. But I'm staring at your ass right now, and I would love to finger it and make you feel good."

"What if it doesn't?"

He kissed me. "It will."

If this were any other guy, I would say no. But Ryker made me do things I never thought I would do. He made me feel things I never expected. "Okay."

He gave me a small smile before he started to thrust into me slowly, his cock sliding through my slickness and reaching as far as it could go. His fingers grazed over my ass cheeks before his index finger slowly pressed into my entrance.

It was a strange sensation, and it was uncomfortable in the beginning. But when he rocked into me from below and watched us move together in the mirror, I forgot how unusual it was. I saw his abundant desire and didn't care about anything else.

He got his two fingers inside me and he slowly pulsed and he thrust at the same time. His cheeks tinted pink and his breathing became deep and rugged. His eyes remained glued to the mirror, and mine remained glued to him. "You have no idea how sexy you look right now."

The ass play didn't bother me, and I felt the typical heat between my legs. I felt the fire scorch me, burning me from the inside out. My hands glided over his chest, and I moved up and down his length, concentrating on his firm jaw and beautiful eyes. I already wanted to come. I could feel it.

My pussy clenched around him, and out of nowhere, the orgasm hit me hard. I dug my nails into his shoulders and felt the most powerful orgasm sweep through me like a hurricane. I screamed through the pleasure and felt my heart stop beating altogether.

Ryker turned away from the mirror and watched me instead. His eyes were glued to my face as he watched me explode, covering his dick with my come. My ass tightened around his fingers as the sensation stretched on forever.

It was the most intense ecstasy I'd ever had, and I didn't know if it was because of the intense fullness or the simple arousal from this man underneath me. But everything was working together to put me into a new plane of pleasure.

His fingers continued to work my ass but he didn't look in the mirror again. All he did was stare at my face as we moved together, man and woman and the abundant lubrication between us. He pressed his face to mine, and he breathed hard with me, burying himself in my tight pussy.

My hands cupped his face, and I looked into his eyes. I felt my heart give way for the man underneath me. I'd never fallen this far for someone, never hit this new level of feeling. I didn't just picture tomorrow and the day after that. I pictured a lifetime into the future of endless nights of good sex and years of joy. I pictured him standing at the end of the altar when Rex gave me away. I pictured our first house outside the city. I pictured giving birth to a son in his exact likeness.

Oh shit.

I really had fallen hard.

He kissed me hard on the mouth, practically bruising my lips as he slid deep inside me repeatedly. "I want to keep going, but fuck, I want to come." His cock was throbbing, pressing against my tight channel anxiously.

"Then come and let's keep going."

He moved his head to the back of the couch and took a deep breath, my words hitting him deep in the gut. "You drive me crazy, you know that?"

"You haven't seen anything yet." Not a single thought possessed me to do this. It was instinct, lust, and even love. I inserted my fingers into his mouth. "Suck."

He straightened and did as I asked, his dark eyes locked to mine the entire time. His tongue moved against my fingers just the way it did against my tongue.

When they were thoroughly wet, I pulled them out and placed them against my entrance, moving his fingers away from the spot.

His eyes immediately went to the mirror.

I inserted my fingers inside myself and pulsed just the way he did to me. I'd never done anything like that in my life, but he made me feel so sexy that I thought I could do anything. I rode his cock and fingered myself at the same time.

"Holy...fuck." He watched my movements in the mirror and his breathing was off the wall. He gripped my hips and pulled me onto his length harder, watching my fingers as they worked my ass.

"Now come."

He squeezed my hips so hard he nearly bruised me. Then he switched into a purely carnal mode and fucked me aggressively. His thighs worked underneath me and pounded his dick into my pussy without an ounce of gentleness. He was officially gone in a fog of unbridled pleasure.

He came with a loud moan, being more vocal than he ever had before. Sweat marked his forehead and he shoved himself farther inside me as he filled my pussy with everything he had. "Fuck. Fuck. Fuck." He gripped my cheeks and pulled them apart as he gave me every single last drop. The orgasm stretched on forever and he held on to it for as long as possible.

When it was finally over, he met my look, his chest rising and falling with his heavy breathing. "That was...perfect." He kissed my neck and then my jawline. When his lips met mine, he gave me a gentle kiss that betrayed the aggression he showed just a moment ago. "I want to fuck you again...just like that."

"Then I'll keep my fingers here...for you to watch."

Like he wasn't just satisfied a moment ago, his eyes darkened again. "You're perfect. You know that?"

I gave him a seductive kiss, my tongue moving with his before I pulled away. "I know."

Ray of Hope

Chapter Thirteen

Rae

I entered the bar and found the girls sitting at a table near the back. Jessie was already in a dress with heels because that's what she wore to work—even though she was on her feet all day. Kayden was in jeans like usual, so she didn't make me stick out like a sore thumb.

They already had my drink waiting for me when I arrived.

"How's the garbage doing?" Jessie asked.

"I work in recycling." She knew better but she liked to tease me whenever possible.

"How's that?" she asked.

"It's good." I didn't get much done today because my mind was in the gutter—thinking about Ryker. "I have something a lot more interesting to talk about."

"That Ryker has an older, richer, and even better looking brother?" Jessie asked with hope bright in her eyes.

"No." Actually, I didn't know if he had any siblings. He was peculiar when it came to the subject of his family—even though I already knew who his father was. "But it is about Ryker."

"What?" Kayden asked. "Did he ask you to move in with him?"

I wish. "No. But...I think I'm in love with him."

Jessie shared a look with Kayden before she rolled her eyes. "We already knew that."

"Yeah," Kayden said. "Old news."

"But now I really know." I sipped my drink and realized Jessie ordered it twice as strong as it needed to be—how she took all of her drinks. "It was looking me in the face the other night."

"What happened?" Kayden asked. "Did he do something particularly romantic?"

I wouldn't call ass play romantic. "You guys know my ass is off limits, right?"

"Yep," Jessie said. "Mine too."

"Mine three," Kayden said.

"Well, we were doing the deed, and I let him finger me a bit." I wouldn't tell this to anyone besides the two of them, not even Zeke. That was just weird.

"Really?" Jessie made a face.

"What was it like?" Kayden asked.

"It was…" I shrugged because I couldn't find the right words. "Just alright. But he went crazy over it. He's always been enthusiastic in bed, but it brought out a completely different side to him."

"So it was totally worth it," Kayden said.

"Absolutely." Seeing him that hot for me made me even hotter.

"He's going to want to fuck you in the ass now." Leave it to Jessie to come out and give it to you straight.

"Totally," Kayden said. "Probably the next time you see him."

"I hope not." A little ass play was okay, but I wasn't ready for nine inches.

"You cave in once, they'll push you," Jessie said. "Been there, done that."

Kayden sipped her drink. "What did he do to make you realize you were in love?"

"Nothing really." There wasn't a specific thing he said or did. It just hit me when we were moving together on that couch. I loved seeing the satisfaction in his eyes, and I wanted to make him feel that good every single day. "I just knew...you know?"

"Awe..." Kayden reached across the table and gave my wrist a gentle squeeze. "I do."

"Are you going to tell him?" Jessie asked.

"I don't know..." I couldn't tell how he felt. Sometimes it seemed like he might feel the same way, but then other times, I remembered how withdrawn he was. He gave me a lot of himself, but not everything.

"I think he feels the same way," Kayden said. "I mean, no guy would stick around as long as he has unless there was more to your relationship than getting his dick wet."

"Me too," Jessie said. "But he might not realize it. Guys are pretty clueless to how they feel."

"So do you think I should tell him?" Talking about this made me nervous in both good and bad ways, so I drank my glass much quicker than I should have. The alcohol was already hitting me.

"I don't know," Kayden said. "You know him better than we do."

"I think you should just tell him," Jessie said. "What's the worst that could happen? He doesn't say it back?"

"That sounds pretty devastating to me," Kayden said with a laugh.

"I agree." That would hurt—a lot.

"Just because he doesn't say it back now doesn't mean he won't later. And he'll know how you feel. I mean, who hates hearing someone say they love them?" Jessie finished her drink then motioned to the waitress to bring another. "I don't think it's a big deal. If anything, it'll boost his ego. And when he's ready, he'll say it because he knows you already feel the same way."

"That's true," Kayden said. "Another way of looking at it."

"So you both think I should tell him?" I asked.

Jessie shrugged. "That's totally up to you. You could wait a while if you want. I mean, there really is no rush to blurt it out right this second."

"But if you're in love, shouldn't you be honest about that?" Kayden asked. "I've never been in love, but if I were, I'd want to be up front about it. You could be yourself, do and say things that you might not otherwise."

"I guess I'll see what happens," I said. "If the right moment comes up, I might say something. But if it doesn't...I'll keep it to myself."

"Problem solved," Kayden said. "Zeke and Rochelle are already saying it to each other and they've only been together for a month. It's been three months with you guys. It's not like it's too soon."

"Yeah, that's true." I thought it was soon because it wasn't like me to feel this strongly about someone. But when I least expected it, it happened. I guarded my heart so securely I didn't think I'd let my walls down enough to feel this way for anyone. But in reality, it really wasn't too soon. "Thanks for giving me your two cents about my love life."

"Always," Kayden said. "We aren't experts by any means, but we've been around the block a few times."

"And I've kissed a lot of frogs," Jessie said. "Ryker is definitely not a frog. Are you sure he doesn't have a brother?"

I chuckled. "I'll ask him next time I see him."

"Thanks so much," Jessie said. "Even a cousin would be okay."

"Got it," I said. "So, enough about me. What's up with you guys?"

***

"Safari, roll over." Rex held the piece of pepperoni and waved it in his face. "Just roll over. Like this." He made the gesture with his hand.

Safari stared at him blankly.

"Come on, boy." Rex whistled then waved the dog treat in his face again.

I rolled my eyes from my seat at the table. "He doesn't need to learn tricks."

"Why not?" Rex asked. "Other dogs do it."

"But Safari is too good for that," I argued. "He gets a treat just for being cute. End of story."

Rex ignored me then tried to teach Safari how to shake.

Safari looked at me with an expression that said, "Can I just have the damn treat?"

Zeke drank his beer while he watched Rex. "Poor dog."

"I know, right?" I drank my beer then turned back to Zeke. "What are we doing tonight?"

"There's an escape room that just opened downtown," Zeke said. "That could be fun. You have to solve a series of puzzles while zombies try to eat your head off."

"Talk about pressure," I said.

"Some friends of mine told me it was cool," he said. "Maybe we should go for it. What's Ryker up to tonight?"

"I haven't talked to him today." I was purposely trying not to be clingy to compensate for the fact I wanted to be with him every second of the day. I wasn't the type of woman to need a man's affection around the clock, but Ryker changed a lot of things about me.

"If we get Ryker, Rochelle, and the girls to come along, that should be enough people. Then we can head to the bars afterward."

I had an excuse to call him, so I took it. I made the call and pressed the phone to my ear.

"Hey." He usually answered with some kind of endearment but he didn't have one today.

"What's up? Are you free tonight?"

"No, I have plans." He didn't elaborate whatsoever, which was very strange.

"Uh, everything alright?" I walked away from the table when Zeke gave me a concerned look. I moved down the hallway until I was finally out of earshot.

"I'm okay," he said. "I'm having a bad day."

I hated to be this kind of girlfriend but I did it anyway. "What are you doing?"

Ryker didn't give me a straightforward answer. "Rae, I'm kinda having some family problems right now. I just want some space."

Selfishly, I felt the sting from being kept out of the loop. He didn't want to tell me his family problems because he never talked about that sort of thing with me. And I was hurt I still wasn't included in that aspect of his life. After the amount of time we'd been together and our obvious closeness, I thought I'd earned the right to know intimate details of his life. But I wouldn't press him on that right now, not when he was clearly upset. "I'm sorry to hear that. You know I'm here if you need anything."

"I do know. Thanks."

"Well…I'll talk to you later." I knew I wouldn't see him all weekend, judging by his tone of voice. I just hoped his absence wouldn't last too long.

"I'll call you on Monday." He hung up without another word.

At least he told me when I could expect to hear from him again.

I walked back into the kitchen, and Zeke's eyes were immediately on me.

"Everything alright?" Zeke asked.

Rex was still wasting his time with Safari.

"Ryker is having some family problems right now," I explained. "He didn't want to talk about it and said he would call me on Monday."

"That's too bad," Zeke said. "Hope it's nothing serious."

"I'm not sure. He doesn't talk about his family to me even though I know his father."

"It's a touchy subject for some people," Zeke said. "I know Ryker resents his dad for making him move to Seattle. Maybe it has something to do with that."

Zeke knew more about it than I did, which was sad. "Yeah, maybe."

He spotted the sadness creep into my eyes. "I wouldn't worry about it. Ryker will come around and everything will be what it was. I wouldn't think about it too much."

"Yeah..." But that was all I could think about until I spoke to Ryker again.

***

The weekend passed slowly because Ryker was on my mind most of the time. I stayed home and spent time with Safari and Rex. Rex knew I was a little down so he wasn't such a pain in the ass.

Out of concern for Ryker, I hoped his family problems weren't serious. Maybe someone got into a car accident but they would recover quickly. Whatever it was, I hoped it was something that wouldn't hurt Ryker. He wasn't an emotional person, but I knew he cared about other people deeply even if he wouldn't admit it.

When I got work on Monday, I tried not to stare at my phone obsessively. Even if he didn't call today, that wouldn't mean anything. I hoped I could sleep over and comfort him in whatever way he needed. Maybe Safari could cheer him up.

After I jogged in the park and had a quick shower, he called.

My heart leapt in joy and I breathed a sigh of relief when I saw his name on the screen. I took a second to compose myself before I answered. "Hey."

"Hey, sweetheart." Like normal, his voice came out deep with a note of confidence—along with possessiveness.

All the tension left my body when I was greeted with his warm attitude. Whatever happened with his family must have resolved itself otherwise he wouldn't be in a good mood. I lay on my bed and stared at the ceiling. "How are you?"

"Good. Just got home from the gym."

"Does that mean you're all hot and sweaty?"

"No." A quiet chuckle escaped through the phone. "But I can get hot and sweaty with you."

"Ooh...that sounds like fun."

"How about you get that fine piece of ass over here then?"

"I'll be there pronto."

"That's my girl."

***

When the elevator doors opened, he was standing there like usual. In his sweatpants and without a shirt, his chest was hard and defined—and ready for my nails to drag down the endless grooves.

I dropped my bag on the floor and immediately moved into his chest. My arms wrapped around his neck, and I kissed him on the lips, telling him how much I missed him through the weekend.

We silently communicated, and he pulled me into his arms just as I tugged on his shoulders and lifted myself until my legs hooked around his waist. We didn't break our kiss, and he carried me into the bedroom. He took his time despite the desperation we both felt. I couldn't wait until my back was pressed against his sheets and he was moving deep inside me.

Ryker crawled up the bed while I dangled underneath him. He set me down with my head against the pillow, and he immediately moved for my clothes. He pulled my jeans and underwear off before he removed his own pants and boxers. His cock was long and ready like it always was when we were together.

He didn't bother taking off my shirt before he shoved himself inside me, stretching me wide and moving through my slickness. I was already wet from the trip to his apartment, thinking about all the dirty things we would do once we were finally reunited.

He hooked my legs over his shoulders and pressed his chest against the back of my thighs. He condensed me tightly, pushing me down until I was curled up underneath him. Then he pounded into me, fucking me hard like we hadn't been together in months rather than days. "I missed you."

My hands glided into his hair, and I fisted the strands as his body slammed into mine. He felt even better than he did before after our time apart, and hearing those words of intimacy made me fall further into the moment. "Missed you so goddamn much."

He moaned against my face and thrust harder, giving me more of this length.

My hands moved to his hips, and I pulled him farther inside me, getting every inch even though it started to hurt when he continued to hit my cervix. I needed as much of him as possible regardless of the pain.

"You didn't touch yourself this weekend, right?"

I was too depressed to feel aroused. The thought didn't even cross my mind. "No. I've been saving myself for you."

He buried himself far inside me with a loud moan then paused, keeping his cock in place for a moment. Then he started up again, but this time, he worked hard and faster, driving us both into a climax that made us moan together, our hands gripping each other tightly as we were overcome with mutual satisfaction and ecstasy.

***

We ate pizza right out of the box on the bed, both naked and hungry. I lay on my stomach with my feet in the air, on my third slice and still hungry. Ryker was propped up on his elbow. He ate a few slices then cut himself off soon after. He sipped a beer then set it on his nightstand.

We hadn't said anything other than discussing what we would have for dinner. And while we ate, we didn't say much either. Sex was the only time we really communicated, even though we didn't say much either.

I wanted to ask about his family but I knew he wouldn't want to talk about it. Ryker was the kind of guy who didn't move even when he was pushed. He was set in his ways and nothing would change his mind. If he wanted me to know, he would tell me.

He stared me down and watched me eat my last slice. "You're the only woman I know who can make eating pizza sexy."

"Why, thank you. It's what I've been striving for my whole life."

He chuckled. "Well, you've accomplished it."

I finished the crust then wiped my fingers with a napkin. I tossed the garbage inside the empty pizza box and tossed it off to the side.

"What did you do this weekend?"

"We went to an escape room downtown."

"How was that?" He scooted closer to me on the bed now that the food was gone.

"Pretty tense. But we cracked the code and got out of there. Then we went to the bars."

"Sounds like a wild night."

"Thankfully, Zeke and Rochelle were there to figure everything out. They're geniuses…"

"Perfect for each other. I really like Rochelle."

"Me too. She's cute."

"And she keeps Zeke occupied so he'll stop obsessing over you."

I kicked him gently. "Don't say that. It's not true."

He smiled like he knew something I didn't.

"You think all my friends are in love with each other."

"Because they are," he said with a laugh. "But I'm glad Zeke is finally moving on. Rochelle is the kind of woman you introduce to your parents. She's a good fit for him."

Zeke never had feelings for me in the first place but I wasn't going to argue with him. Instead, I concentrated on the positive part of his sentence. "I like Rochelle too. Rex is weird about her, but Rex is just an oddball."

Ryker raised an eyebrow. "What problem could he possibly have with her?"

"Says they're moving too fast. Already introducing each other to parents and saying the L word. I don't see what the big deal is. If Zeke has found the one, what does it matter if they've only been seeing each other for a month?"

"There's more to this story than Rex lets on. Because his discrimination doesn't make any sense."

I rolled my eyes. "Rex is an idiot so I wouldn't think about it too hard. Scientists still can't figure him out."

Ryker slowly moved on top of me and kissed my back, pressing his lips all the way down my spine until he reached my ass. He kept going, moving lower until he reached my pussy.

I closed my eyes and enjoyed it, forgetting everything we were just talking about.

His lips moved back up again, sprinkling affection on me until he reached the back of my neck. He straddled my ass during his movements then pressed his cock between my crack again. He slid his mouth to my ear and breathed deeply, his excitement obvious in the way he breathed.

He pointed his cock at my entrance and slowly slid inside, moaning quietly as he entered me. "I can't wait to fuck that tiny asshole." He slid all the way inside then held himself on his arms, his chest pressed to my back. He thrust into me hard, pinning me to the sheets as he grinded against my ass. "But this wet pussy is just as good." He fucked me from behind slowly, giving me long and even stokes.

His weight pushed me into the sheets, and I felt my clitoris rub against the bunched up bedding underneath me. It felt incredible, and I just had to lie there and enjoy it. Ryker craned his neck and kissed my shoulders and my jawline, his breathing coming out deep and sexy.

I turned my face and pressed myself into the side of his neck. "Ryker…"

He picked up his pace slightly. "Sweetheart." He moved into me for a long time, making me come along the way. He never picked up his speed because he was taking his time, making it last as long as possible.

Then we switch positions, and he rolled me to my back. He hooked the back of my knees in the crooks of his arms and entered me from above. He gave me his entire length with the same pace, shaking my tits with every thrust.

He looked like a god above me, claiming what was his to own and rule. He pounded into me like I was his private possession to enjoy for the rest of the time. Sweat formed on his chest, and the glistening of his muscles made him look even sexier.

He was going to make me come again. I could feel it.

Ryker locked his eyes with mine and watched my reactions. He concentrated on my eyes as well as my lips, noticing when I bit my lip from time to time. Sometimes, I whispered his name, and his eyes darkened.

My nails dug into his arms, and I held on as he continued to ram his cock deep inside me. I was always wet for him so his cock slid in with ease. He still stretched me anyway because my pussy would never get used to his size.

"You look so beautiful right now..." His blue eyes were darker in color, appearing gray. Sweat formed on his forehead and dripped down his temple. He breathed hard through the exertion, his powerful chest expanding with every breath he took.

My fingers dug into his biceps, and I felt myself get swept away with the man who was pounding into me. I couldn't go a weekend without missing him, and I probably couldn't even last a day. My heart had been swept away a long time ago. I couldn't recall the exact moment, but it happened sometime in the past. I didn't want to hide it anymore, the way I felt about this man who had become so much more than a one-night stand. "Ryker...I love you."

He continued to move into me but his pace immediately slowed. His cock was still hard but the desperation to come was no longer in his eyes. His gaze was locked to mine, but instantly, his look was masked and impossible to decipher. He closed off from me immediately, no longer lost in the moment.

And he didn't say it back.

He broke eye contact with me altogether and leaned farther over me. He pounded into me hard, like he was trying to finish as quickly as possible. I didn't come even though I normally would have, and he finished with a quiet moan that hardly escaped his lips.

He stayed on top of me after he finished and caught his breath. When he leaned down to kiss me, it felt like that granny kiss we exchanged on our first real date. It was passionless and empty.

Then he pulled out of me and immediately walked into the bathroom. The water turned on a moment later, and I heard the glass door shut behind him once he was inside.

I stayed in the same spot where he left me and stared at the ceiling. Regret washed over me when I realized I said something I couldn't take back. For a moment, I actually thought he would say it back. Was I stupid for ever thinking he would?

I didn't like the way he walked away from me without saying a word. He jumped in the shower and turned on the water to drown out all the noise. But at the same time, I couldn't blame him for searching for some privacy. I just dropped a bomb on him that he clearly wasn't able to handle.

I wished I could turn back time and erase what just happened.

I wished I never told him.

***

I could have just gone home when he was in the shower, but I didn't want to run away from my problems. It would be awkward until we talked about it. Once we got that out of the way, it would be over with. And after a week or so, we would be back to normal.

I sat on the couch and watched TV wearing one of his old t-shirts. The Fresh Prince of Bel-Air was on, and I needed something good to cheer me up. But it didn't matter how many times I saw Carlton dance—I still felt like shit.

After he got out of the shower, he stayed in his room for a while. My bag was still in there so he knew I hadn't left. After about an hour, he walked down the hallway and made an appearance. He was dressed in his sweatpants and a t-shirt.

He stood behind the other couch with his hands resting against the back of the chair. He stared at the opposite wall where the mirror was and didn't look at me.

I decided to break the ice. "I know this is awkward, and I'm sorry for making it that way. But I don't regret what I said or feeling this way. I got lost in the moment and it slipped out. But I want you to know you don't need to say it back. I won't be upset if you don't. There's no pressure at all."

He didn't have a single reaction. His eyes were glued to his own visage in the mirror.

"I'm not upset with you, and I hope you aren't upset with me."

Still nothing.

Now I didn't know what to do. He'd completely closed off from me.

I sighed. "Do you want me to leave?"

He bowed his head and looked down at his own feet. "No."

"Then can we just move on from this?"

"I guess."

I hoped he would give me a more thorough explanation of his behavior, but he obviously wasn't going to. "Well…do you want to watch a movie or something?"

Like he hadn't heard my question at all, he said something else. "Were you expecting me to say it back?" He finally looked at me for the first time since the incident. The expression in his eyes was different, ghostly.

"I thought you might, I guess."

"Why?"

The question caught me off guard—because it hurt so much. "I see the way you look at me. I see the way we are together. And I started to feel this way a while ago. I don't think it's ridiculous to assume you might feel the same way. I know you're quiet and intense, but you aren't a robot."

He bowed his head again.

"Again, I'm not upset if you don't say it back."

He tapped his fingers against the back of the couch.

"Nothing has to change. Let's stop talking about it and move on."

He dropped his hands away from the couch and walked toward the kitchen. His shoulders were tenser than I'd ever seen them. "Want anything?"

"No, thanks."

He was gone for a while, probably enjoying a beer by himself in the kitchen before he had to face me again. When he returned, it was nearly five minutes later. He sat on the couch beside me but he didn't show me an ounce of affection. His hand didn't move to my thigh, and he didn't even look at me.

Did I just ruin everything?

Chapter Fourteen

Rae

"Why do you look like shit?" Rex stood at the kitchen counter eating a bowl of cereal even though it was five in the afternoon.

"Because I feel like shit." I slammed the door behind me and walked right past Safari without even looking at him.

"Are you sick?" Rex blurted. "Because I can't get sick right now. I need to be at Groovy Bowl every day, and I don't have health insurance so if I catch something—"

"I'm not sick." Damn, he wouldn't shut up sometimes.

"Then what's up?"

"Nothing." I walked into my bedroom and shut the door. Once I was alone, I tossed my purse aside and fell onto my bed, grateful to have some privacy to throw myself a pity party. I stared at the ceiling then closed my eyes.

Rex knocked before he opened the door. Safari immediately darted inside then jumped on the bed. He snuggled into my side and rested his chin on my belly, knowing something was wrong because he knew me so well. "Everything alright?"

"I'm fine," I said with a sigh. "I just want to be alone right now."

Rex continued to stand in the doorway, confused as to what he should do.

"Really, I'm fine. You can go."

"I can tell something is really wrong." He leaned against the doorframe and crossed his arms over his chest. "And I know you need someone right now."

"You're overreacting. I just had a bad day."

"I've never seen you ignore Safari." He nodded toward the dog curled into my side. "I know it was more than just a bad day. So talk to me."

I'd talk to Jessie and Kayden later…if then. "It's really nothing—"

"Shut up and talk to me. I won't give you shit for the entire conversation. I promise." He walked into the room and sat on the small armchair next to my nightstand. He crossed his arms again and slumped into the chair.

"You don't care, Rex. And that's perfectly fine."

"Rae, you know I care." He gave me a thoughtful expression, a sight I rarely saw.

I sat up and rested my back against the headboard. "I did something really stupid with Ryker..."

Rex held his tongue and didn't crack any jokes like he promised.

"I told him I loved him, and he didn't say it back. It's been awkward ever since..." I dragged my face down my hands in frustration. I should have kept my mouth shut but I was a dumbass and didn't think.

Rex could have made a mean comment, saying I told you so. He warned me Ryker wouldn't give me what I wanted but he didn't do a victory dance. "Have you talked to him about it?"

"Yeah. I told him it didn't matter if he said it back or not. I wasn't upset and he shouldn't be either."

"And?"

"We didn't talk about it again, but things are still awkward."

Rex looked at Safari beside me and fell quiet with his thoughts.

"I thought he would say it back because of the way he treats me. I'm hurt he didn't, but I don't think it's the end of the world. I just hope he understands that it's nothing to be uncomfortable about."

"As long as you told him it was okay, it shouldn't be a big deal. Give it a few weeks, and things will go back to normal."

"You think?" I couldn't stop my tone of hope from escaping.

"I'm sure it'll be fine. I mean, he must feel really uncomfortable by what you said. But with enough time, he'll stop thinking about it. If some woman I was seeing said the same to me, I'd be weird about it too."

"Even if she were your girlfriend?"

"It doesn't matter who she is. If I don't feel the same way, it's going to be strange no matter what."

"I guess…"

Rex eyed me, his brotherly affection coming through. "I'm sorry he doesn't feel the same way."

"It's okay…"

"But that doesn't mean he won't someday."

"I know. I'm okay with that. I just hope he doesn't push me away because of it."

"I wouldn't worry about it. Give him some space for right now. But he'll come around."

I clung to Rex's words because I needed to believe them. I hoped my confession didn't put our relationship in jeopardy. Even though we hit a rough patch, that didn't mean I wanted us to go separate ways. Ryker was still the man I loved, and I wanted to be the woman he loved someday.

***

I gave Ryker space for a few days before I finally caved. Three days had gone by and I didn't hear a peep from him. Not even a dirty text message or a dick pic. I'd gotten a few of those from him, and I actually liked what I saw.

But now it was silent.

My impatience got the best of me so I sent him a message. *Mariners are on in an hour. Want to come over and watch it?* Knowing Rex would be there might make him more comfortable. If my brother was around, there wouldn't be any serious conversations or overwhelming affection.

His three dots popped up on the screen. *Sure.*

I finally released the breath I was holding. *See you then.*

I left my bedroom and walked into the hallway. "Ryker is coming over to watch the game."

"That's great." Rex seemed truly enthused by that information. He'd never been so excited to see Ryker come over as my boyfriend. "When?"

"About an hour."

"Alright. I'm glad to hear it."

"You can't mention anything we talked about. Act normal."

"Got it." He gave me a thumbs up.

"Rex, I mean it. No pulling him into the corner and whispering threats in his ear."

Rex rolled his eyes. "Dude, that happened one time."

"It happened twice," I snapped. "And there won't be a third time."

"Fine. I'll behave."

"Thank you."

"Should I invite anyone else?" he asked. "Make it more normal? Kayden probably isn't doing anything…"

"Nah. Let's just leave it as the three of us."

He didn't hide his frown at the comment. "Alright…"

***

When Ryker knocked on the door, Rex immediately looked at me on the couch. "Should I get it?"

"No." I walked to the door with Safari on my heels. I opened the door and saw him standing on the other side, in jeans and a thick black jacket. It'd been raining for the past hour. "Hey."

"Hey." He gave me a somewhat fond look, but it was nothing in comparison to the looks he used to give me. He stepped inside and wiped his dirty shoes on the rug. Instead of greeting me with a kiss or a hug, he turned to Safari. "Hey, boy." He patted him on the head. "Long time, no see."

It's been long time, no see for us too, but whatever. "Beer?"

"Sure." He walked into the living room.

No kiss. No hug. Nothing.

This was such a goddamn nightmare.

"What's up?" Ryker greeted Rex with a restrained form of enthusiasm.

"Pissed," Rex barked.

No. No. No.

Rex continued on. "The Mariners are getting their asses handed to them. Like, didn't they go to school for this?"

"To play professional baseball?" Ryker asked with a laugh. "I don't think so."

"Well, that makes sense now. No wonder why they suck."

Thank god Rex was on his best behavior. I grabbed the beers and walked into the living room. To my annoyance, Ryker was sitting on the couch with Rex. If I wanted to sit with him, I'd have to squeeze in between the two guys and that simply wasn't comfortable. Did he do it on purpose? I handed the beer over.

"Thanks." He twisted off the cap with his hand and took a drink.

I sat on the other couch, and Safari immediately jumped up beside me. I hid my irritation at Ryker's behavior. He was purposely keeping me at a distance and doing everything possible to keep space between us. But if that was how he felt, why did he come over in the first place?

We spent the next few hours watching the game, and empty beer bottles piled up on the table. Safari snuggled closer to me. With his powerful dog sense, he knew I was battling my anger.

It seemed like Ryker loosened up a bit toward the end of the game. He and Rex were making jokes of the opposing team and then talking about the recent events inside Groovy Bowl. There was a lot of shit talk back and forth, normal banter between two friends.

But Ryker didn't talk to me once.

I couldn't believe all of this was happening just because I said three little words.

Three stupid words.

When the game was over, Ryker gathered his beer bottles and tossed them in the trash in the kitchen. He was out of sight so Rex turned to me.

Rex mouthed, "What the hell?"

I shrugged. "I don't know," I mouthed back.

"I think I'm gonna take off," Ryker announced from the kitchen.

Rex nodded his head toward the door. "Talk to him." He pointed to the entryway while he still mouthed to me.

This was stupid. I couldn't believe it was really happening. "Alright. I'll walk you out." I walked to the front door and saw him already standing there in his thick coat. "Too bad they lost. But it was a good game."

"Yeah. They'll still get into the playoffs so it's fine."

"I hope so. If not, Rex will murder someone."

He chuckled. "Rex is too stupid to figure that out."

"Hey," Rex snapped. "Maybe I'm stupid but not deaf."

Ryker opened the door and stepped out in one fluid motion. "I'll talk to you later."

Again, no kiss. No hug. Nothing. "Alright."

He nodded before he walked down the hall and disappeared into the stairway.

I shut the door then leaned my back against it, feeling defeated, frustrated, and flat out pissed off.

Rex rounded the corner with a grim look on his face. "Sorry, sis…" He only referred to me that way when he really did feel bad for me.

"I want to slap him—really hard."

"Maybe you should."

"I don't regret what I said because I meant it. I still mean it now. But he shouldn't behave this way. It's absolutely ridiculous."

He crossed his arms over his chest and leaned against the counter. "Yeah, it is…"

"What should I do?"

Rex shrugged with his large shoulders. "I really don't know, Rae. I've never been in this situation before."

"He's gonna dump me, isn't he?" It was only a matter of time before he cut me loose. He'd already shut me out completely, treated me like a friend, and would hardly look at me. We were so close just a week ago, and now it seemed like that connection never happened.

"I wouldn't say that."

"But he is. It's so damn obvious."

"I would give him a little more space and see what he does. And if he still acts like a little bitch, I'd confront him."

I stared at the ground as I felt the hopelessness sink in. "I just want this to go away."

"It will. All things come to pass."

It was the wisest phrase I'd ever heard him say, but now wasn't the time for a compliment. "Nothing is worse than being shut out like this. I would much rather him yell at me than give me the cold shoulder. I don't deserve it."

"No, you don't." He nodded in agreement.

I couldn't believe this was happening. Just a week ago, I was happy and in love. And now...I was totally miserable.

***

I gave him an entire week to contact me and he never did. He never texted me, called me, or stopped by the apartment. My despair quickly turned to rage for being ignored like this. He acted like I did something terrible to him, lied to him or cheated on him. All I did was tell him how I really felt.

Was that really so terrible?

"I'm gonna march over there and give him a piece of my mind." I snatched my coat from the coatrack and stormed to the entryway.

"Whoa, hold on." Rex abandoned his dinner at the table and rushed to my side. "Not a good plan. Abort."

"It's been a week, Rex. He's ignored me for an entire week."

"Yeah, he's an ass. I get it. But catching him off guard and screaming at him isn't going to help anything."

"I don't give a shit anymore." I nudged Rex out of the way and walked into the hallway. "No one treats me like this and gets away with it. I've been patient for two weeks but no more."

This time Rex didn't stop me. "Then give him hell."

***

I knew the code to get into his apartment so I used it. It wasn't exactly ethical, but if he hadn't ignored me and pissed me off, this wouldn't have happened.

The elevator rose to the top floor and came to a stop. Then the doors opened.

The living room was empty but all the lights were on so I assumed he was home. When he heard the elevator ding, he came down the hallway, unease in his eyes when he realized someone was in his apartment. He stopped in his tracks when he realized it was me.

I didn't issue any kind of apology. I stepped inside and heard the doors shut behind me. His features were difficult to decipher, because once again, he was an enigma. He wasn't a man who just came out and said what he was thinking. "I told you I loved you. I meant it when I said it, and I still mean it now."

He rested his arms by his sides, but his shoulders were tense.

"When I said I wouldn't be upset if you didn't say it back, I meant that too. Our relationship doesn't have to change, but for some reason, you've completely cut me off like I don't matter to you. I never hear from you, and the one time we're together, you avoid me like I have a disease. Ryker, this is absolutely ridiculous."

His eyes were lidded and cold, complete masked.

"I'm not putting up with it anymore. I've given you two weeks to get your ass into gear, but it seems like things are getting worse rather than better. I'm not sure why confessing how I feel would be so offensive that you would treat me like that. But it's unacceptable." I stepped farther into his apartment, and he didn't take a step back. "So is this over? If it is, be a man and dump me. Don't ignore me until I go away."

Ryker barely blinked as he stared me down. His chest hardly rose so it wasn't clear if he was even breathing. His hands were slack by his sides and he didn't make fists. Even now, he wasn't giving me anything.

I waved a hand in front of his face. "Anyone home?"

That finally provoked him into saying something. "Rae, this isn't working out. We had fun while it lasted, but it's time we call it quits."

When I told him to dump me like a real man, I didn't think he would actually do it. I thought confronting him would make him realize he'd been a dick and then he would apologize. The idea of us being over just because of what I said was ridiculous. "Because I told you I love you?" The hurt remained out of my voice, and I took on an incredulous tone to mask my pain.

"We're in different places. I can't be with someone who's not in the same place."

"Ryker, we've been dating for three months. Pigs fall in love quicker than that. Love is just a feeling. It's not an expectation or a commitment. I told you I'm okay with you not feeling the same way."

His tone darkened. "But I'm never going to feel the same way."

Those words cut me like a knife.

"Ever."

Unnecessary use of force. "I don't believe that. I think you do love me but you aren't ready to admit it."

"Rae, I don't. I really, truly don't."

Despite how aggressively he spoke, I still didn't believe him. I remembered our relationship from beginning to end. I remembered how a one-night stand turned into something more. I remembered the way he touched me, kissed me, and all the pretty words he said. I remembered how jealous he used to get. I remembered everything, down to the last detail. "I can't believe this..."

"Well, you better start."

I did nothing to deserve this cruelty, not a damn thing. And I didn't appreciate it. "You're talking to me like I did something terrible to you."

"You broke into my apartment."

"Because you ignored me."

"If you'd called, I would have answered."

"And danced around the subject and kept me at a distance, like always." We'd had our fights before but they were nothing like this. He was a stranger I didn't know. He was an evil man intent on hurting me as much as possible. "And you wouldn't have called me because you're a damn pussy, Ryker. You tried to ignore me like I would just go away. Like the past three months could have just disappeared."

His eyes narrowed to slits.

"I don't know what happened to you, Ryker. But saying those three little words doesn't deserve these kind of repercussions. You have your own issues that you aren't telling me. There's something else going on that you're hiding from me. If you don't want to tell me, fine. But I'm not sticking around for more of this nonsense."

His mouth was shut like he had nothing else to say.

I turned to the elevator and walked inside. I hit the button to the first floor and stared at him, waiting for him to pull his head out of his ass and realize he was being a goddamn idiot. The doors began to close but he still didn't do anything.

Finally, he spoke. "Goodbye, Rae."

The doors shut.

The elevator started to move, and I gripped the rail for support. I put on a nice show because I refused to appear weak to a man who clearly didn't respect me. I leaned against the door and closed my eyes, feeling hot tears forming behind my eyelids. I refused to let them fall because I was stronger than that.

I was too strong for a weak man like him.

***

I knocked on the door and listened to his footsteps inside the house.

Zeke opened the door and didn't hide his surprise at my appearance on his doorstep. He was in sweatpants and a t-shirt, clearly relaxing in front of the TV after a long day at work. He glanced past me to see if I was alone. "Hey, what's up?"

"Is Rochelle here?"

"No." His eyes narrowed in surprise. "Why?"

That was a loaded question. "I just got into a fight with Ryker and...I don't know. For some reason, my feet brought me here." I didn't want to go home and listen to Rex say he told me so. I didn't want to tell Jessie and Kayden what happened and see them gasp in shock. I didn't want to sit alone in my room, trapped with my disturbing thoughts. Zeke was the most comforting person I knew. He was always there for me without a judgmental tone. He'd always been a good friend to me since the day we met. And for whatever reason, I felt innately comfortable with him.

Zeke didn't press his questions on me. "Come inside." He opened the door wide and guided me through, his arm moving around my waist. He shut the door then walked with me into the living room. The TV was on so he quickly hit the mute button. Most of the blinds were closed except on the large doors that led to his backyard. A field of green with trees sat right behind the porch. Zeke's place always smelled like pine needles and freshly cut wood. Somehow, it comforted me.

He sat beside me on the couch and stared into my face. "What happened?"

I told him the story from the beginning, from the day I told Ryker I loved him until what happened thirty minutes ago.

Zeke didn't say anything but his jaw clenched in anger. His eyes weren't comforting any longer. There was rage deep inside, unstoppable and hot anger.

"I know Ryker was pissed I barged into his apartment like that, and I understand why. In a few weeks, I think he'll come back to me and apologize for everything. So I'm not really sure if we're broken up or not."

"If you aren't, then you better dump him now."

I watched the fire dance in his eyes.

"Rae, this is ridiculous. Who reacts that way? You told him you loved him and he treated you like shit." Zeke wasn't normally this aggressive but he clearly snapped. "If any guy is lucky enough to have you feel that way about him, then he should be dancing on the goddamn table. He should be screaming those words back to you. He should ask himself how he got so lucky to have the love of such an amazing woman. He shouldn't be a fucking dickhead and act like a sophomore in high school. Fuck that guy."

Damn, he was pissed.

Zeke read the wary expression on my face and realized he wasn't helping. "Sorry…I got carried away."

"It's okay."

"I won't take back what I said. Honestly, he's not good enough for you, Rae."

"Yeah…"

He wrapped his arm around my shoulder and pulled me into his side.

I rested my head on his shoulder and closed my eyes.

"I'm sorry you feel like this. I wish I could fix it."

"You're doing a great job, Zeke. I do feel better."

He rubbed my back gently as he rested his head against mine. "You don't deserve this, Rae. There are men out there who would never make you feel this way. There are men better than Ryker."

"I know…Rochelle is so lucky to have you."

He flinched under my words, but only slightly. If I wasn't lying on him, I wouldn't have even noticed.

"You're such a good guy, Zeke. You would never hurt anyone. Always so respectful, humble, and honest. Maybe you should teach a class or something. Teach men how to be men." I'd seen Zeke with Rochelle, and he was so thoughtful and committed. He would never hurt her. He would never hurt anyone.

"Maybe," he said with a forced chuckle.

I let the minutes trickle by as I listened to his beating heart. Concentrating on that rhythmic sound brought me some form of comfort. "I don't know why I always go for the wrong guys. I'm programmed to fall for assholes. It's in my DNA."

"One day, you'll find the right guy. I know you will."

"Even now...I still love him." Saying those words out loud nearly shattered me. Only because Zeke was there did I keep my emotions in check. "I don't know why. I don't know how to explain it. But I do..."

He ran his hand down my back. "Love is a tricky thing."

"I think he'll get his act together in a few weeks. He'll apologize...and I'll forgive him."

"Rae, I know it's not my place, but I really don't think you should do that."

"I completely agree with you. But I can't change the way I feel. I know if he got on his knees and apologized to me, I would take him back. I would buy all of his excuses just for the chance to be happy again...because what we had was pretty incredible."

Zeke didn't press his argument further because he knew he wouldn't change my mind. I was stuck in a painful web of emotions and nothing I did would pull me back out. I was at Ryker's mercy even though it was painful to admit that truth.

"I understand how you feel. When you feel this strongly about someone you can't always think straight. You're a slave to everything they do. You tell yourself to walk away but it's so hard. You keep hoping. You keep dreaming." He pulled his face away so he could look at me. "And nothing they do will ever change the way you feel about them."

I thought he was talking about Rochelle, but that didn't quite add up. There was no reason for him to walk away from Rochelle. She seemed to be the perfect person for him, and it was obvious she loved him because she couldn't keep her eyes off him. "I didn't know you ever felt that way about someone."

He broke eye contact. "It was a long time ago."

"You loved her but she didn't love you?" Since he brought it up, I thought it was okay to ask questions.

"Basically."

"I'm sorry, Zeke."

"It's okay. I got through it, and you'll get through this too."

"Yeah…I hope so."

He continued to rub my back with a look of concern in his eyes. "You want to sleep here tonight? The spare bedroom is all yours."

"No, I should probably go home. Rex will worry about me. He saw the way I stormed out like a madwoman."

"I know that look," he said with a smile. "It wouldn't be smart to get in your way."

"He's probably worrying about me right now. I just don't feel like talking about it with him."

"Then why did you talk to me?"

"I don't know," I whispered. "I guess Rex warned me that Ryker was a mistake. I'll have to admit he was right, and he's going to rub it in my face."

His voice came out gentle. "Rae, he would never do that."

"Yes, he would. And you know what? He has every right. I should have listened to him."

"Even if he was right, Rex didn't want to be right." Zeke dropped his hand from my back and rested it on his thigh. "I knew it would be a mistake too, but I wanted Ryker to prove me wrong. We all did. None of us feel any sense of victory. All we care about is how you feel right now."

I finally cracked a smile. "I'm so lucky to have you guys…wouldn't know what to do without you."

He leaned toward me and pressed his lips against my temple. It was the kind of affection he'd never given me before, and the comfort it provided was something I couldn't explain. My heart stopped aching for once, and all I felt was joy. "You'll never have to."

Ray of Hope

Chapter Fifteen

Rex

I worried about Rae all night.

This was the kind of shit I tried to protect her from. The woman had been through enough. We'd both been through enough. We paid our dues and now it was time for us to be happy. I knew Ryker wouldn't respect her the way he promised he would. I knew he would break her heart somewhere down the road.

And now it happened.

I teased my sister a lot because she was annoying, like every other sister in the world. But she truly was one of the best people I knew. She took me in and had my back no matter what. If someone gave me shit, she'd be the first person to jump in the fight and tell them off. But she was also the first person to give me shit in the first place. It didn't make any sense, but it worked for us.

I took care of her when we were growing up, and the second she was stable, she started to take care of me. She invested money into my bowling alley so I could get back on my feet, and she was still giving me a place to live with food on the table. She was my biggest supporter, the one person in the world I could rely on no matter how angry we were with each other.

That was real love.

And the idea of someone taking advantage of her good nature, her optimism, and her heart just ticked me off.

I wanted to march over there and beat the shit out of Ryker myself.

So fucking much.

But I knew Rae wouldn't want that. She would want me to stand on the sidelines and keep my insults to myself. She wouldn't want me to fight her battles for her because she could fight them on her own.

After midnight, she finally came home.

I jumped off the couch and nearly tripped over the armrest as I tried to get to her as quickly as possible. "What happened?"

She gave me a sad look that clearly said, "Nothing good."

"I'm sorry, Rae. Really, I am."

She told me what happened, that Ryker was a huge dick then she went to Zeke's place so he could comfort her. Then she came home when she felt a little better.

There were so many things I wanted to say, but I knew it was better to keep them to myself. It blew my mind that Ryker could date her that long and then turn on her with the snap of a finger. He treated her like she cheated on him or something. In reality, she just confessed how much she cared about him.

My sister's eyes sagged with exhaustion mixed with despair. She couldn't put on a brave face in front of me anymore. She wore her heart on her sleeve, her bruises on her skin. "I think he'll come back to me and apologize in a few weeks. At least, that's what I hope he does."

I couldn't believe she would even consider forgiving him. My sister didn't put up with bullshit, so I couldn't understand why she was putting up with this. But getting in her face right now wouldn't do any good. She needed a friend right now. She needed somewhere she felt safe. "I'm sorry, Rae." I kept repeating myself but there were no other words to fit the moment.

"I guess you were right..." She sighed in defeat when she looked at me. "I should have listened to you, Rex."

I felt like shit for being right. I wished a million times over that I was dead wrong. I wished Ryker had been everything I claimed he wasn't and swept Rae off her feet and became her Prince Charming. "That's not true. Don't say that."

"It is. And we both know it." She walked to her bedroom down the hall with Safari on her trail.

Should I go after her and talk to her? Or should I just leave her alone? I didn't know what to do.

After standing there for a few minutes, I finally decided to go into her room. "I'm always here to talk, Rae. I just want you to know that."

She was lying in bed with Safari beside her, her back turned to me. "I know."

"Is there something I can do? I can pick you up something from Mega Shake." It was her favorite place. Anytime she needed cheering up, that's the first place I headed.

She didn't turn around or sit up. She continued to lay in bed in the clothes she'd been wearing, her dog tucked into her side for comfort. "No, thanks, Rex. I'm not hungry."

"Alright..."

"I'll be fine." Her voice came out surprisingly steady. "I just want to be alone right now."

"Okay." The one thing I could believe in her was her strength. She'd been through a lot and always made it back on top. She'd fallen hard now, but she had the spirit to crawl back up. She always did and always would. "I know you'll be okay, Rae. You always are."

***

"I'm gonna slap him so hard his neck is going to snap off." Jessie ignored her drink altogether because she was so ticked. She hadn't had a sip when she would normally be on her third or fourth by now.

Kayden didn't touch her drink either. Instead of being venomously angry like Jessie, she was quiet with sadness. "Poor Rae...she doesn't deserve this."

"No. She doesn't." Zeke rested his arm over the back of the booth and stared across the bar, his eyes seeing something in the distance. He was in quiet contemplation, thinking about the drama that surrounded someone he cared about. "It doesn't add up. Why would a woman saying she loves you bother you that much?" He turned back to us, his eyes filling with anger. "I can understand why it would be awkward for a while, but to dump her? It doesn't make any sense."

"I don't get it either," I said. "They're just words. They don't change the relationship that much. It's not like she would say it every day or something."

"And she even said he wasn't obligated to say it back," Jessie said. "She gave him an out. It's not like she gave him an ultimatum."

"She told me he said he would never love her," Zeke said. "And that's why he couldn't be with her. But even then, that doesn't make sense."

"Damn," Kayden said. "That's harsh."

"No," Jessie said. "That's just an asshole thing to say."

Zeke shook his head. "It's been so hard for me not to call him and give him a piece of my mind."

"It's been hard for me not to wait by his car and jump him." I'd fantasized about it a few times. Too many times.

"And the worst part is," Zeke said. "Rae said she thinks he'll come around in a few weeks after he cools off. He'll apologize and say he didn't mean any of it. And then they'll be back to where they were."

Kayden shook her head. "I wouldn't forgive him after that. Too hateful."

"I don't think he's going to come back," Jessie said. "You don't say stuff like that to someone and then ask for another chance."

"I hope he doesn't come back," I said. "It took a lot for Zeke and me to give him a chance the first time. No way he's getting a redo."

"No fucking way," Zeke said.

"Where is Rae now?" Kayden asked.

"She's at home watching TV," I said. "She said she wanted some space, and I thought I'd let you guys know so she doesn't have to do it herself. It was already hard enough for her to tell Zeke and me."

"I get it," Jessie said. "I want to hug her or something. But I'm sure she wants to be alone right now."

"I'm gonna send her flowers tomorrow," Kayden said. "Write her a cute note."

"Maybe we should all give her flowers," Zeke said. "Remind her that we all love her even if Ryker doesn't."

"That's a good idea," I said. "How much do flowers cost?" I was still broke.

Zeke already knew what I was going to ask. "I'll take care of it, Rex. Just sign the card."

I patted him on the shoulder. "Thanks, man. I'll pay you back soon enough."

"I know," he answered. "I'll just add it to your tab."

Ray of Hope

Chapter Sixteen

Rae

Two weeks had come and gone, and I didn't hear anything from Ryker.

I expected him to contact me with an apology at some point. I expected him to realize what he lost when he cruelly dumped me like I never meant a damn thing to him. I expected him to realize it was just a horrible mistake.

But he never did.

Rex watched me like a hawk during the past two weeks. He even had dinner waiting when I came home, and magically, the apartment was clean. He couldn't figure it out for the past year he'd been living there, but the second I went through a hard time, he stepped up.

Since it was sweet, I didn't give him shit about it.

Everyone came to my apartment almost every day. They dropped by for no reason at all, to either play games or watch TV with me. Kayden and Jessie never asked about Ryker, and that's how I knew Rex and Zeke already filled them in.

In fact, no one asked me about him.

No one asked how I was doing or how I was holding up.

No one gave me looks of pity.

They treated me like everything was normal, and that kind of comfort was exactly what I needed. If they kept pestering me about how I was doing, then I would never stop thinking about it. This was a much better approach.

Rochelle didn't come around, and I assumed it was because Zeke wanted it just to be our group. He didn't need to do that because I really liked Rochelle. She was a woman, so I was sure she had her own experiences with heartbreak.

We played a game of Scattergories at the table, and I finally won a round. Zeke had won all the others. "Yes! Take that, losers."

"Such a gracious winner…" Jessie covered her smile by sipping her wine.

"I'm tired of losing to Zeke all the time." I tossed the cards back into the box and set up a new game. "Someone needed to take the torch away from him."

"So this is personal." He rested his elbows on the table, showing off his nice arms under his long sleeved shirt. He wore a Mariners hat, and looked like every other sports fan in the city. The look he gave me was playful but also competitive.

"I think I speak for everyone when I say we're tired of you winning all the time." No one likes an overachiever.

"I never win," Rex said. "I'm too dumb."

"Hey, that's not true." Kayden's voice came rushing out like a mother consoling her son. "You're the smartest guy I know." Her hand immediately moved to his upper arm. "You're just good at different things than we are."

He glanced down at her arm and smiled. "I guess that's true…"

She quickly pulled her hand away like she'd suddenly been burned. "Alright. Let's get the next game going. I'll make some margaritas."

I knew I lost the man I loved and it was still difficult to accept. If he hadn't come back by now, then he wasn't going to. But in the face of adversity, I realized just how lucky I was. I had a group of friends that were family, and they were there for me in the best way possible, just the way I was there for them. Even in the darkness, there was light. And I realized I had personal suns that would follow me everywhere I went—always keeping me warm.

***

It was the first time I had the energy to get dressed up and go out. Jessie bought me a dress at her favorite clothing store and asked me to wear it. It really was beautiful, a short black dress with a nearly open back. She knew my size and shape, and she knew how to make anyone look good.

Zeke came to the table with another lemon drop in his hand. He placed it beside my nearly empty glass. "It looks like you need a refill." He stood at the high top beside me, wearing a collared shirt and jeans.

"Thank you but you don't need to be my personal drink fetcher." He'd been doing it all night, making sure I never ran empty.

"Hey. Friends never let friends go thirsty."

I sipped it before I returned it to the table. "Well, thank you. It's delicious."

"You're welcome. But I can't take credit for making it."

"But you did carry it over here. It probably got tastier on the way."

He gave me that charming smile that made all the girls melt. "True."

"Where's Rochelle?"

"Oh, she had plans tonight."

I knew he was lying. I could see it clearly in his eyes. "Zeke, you don't have to stop bringing her around just to make me feel better about being alone. I can watch you guys be in love, and I'm perfectly fine with it." Whenever I saw Zeke with Rochelle, I wished Ryker would love me like that. Of course, the thought crossed my mind along with an overwhelming amount of jealousy. But I wanted Zeke to be happy, and he shouldn't have to tone it down just because I was miserable. "I like Rochelle. I think she's a great addition to the group."

Zeke finally dropped his act. "Alright. I will."

"Thank you." The poor girl shouldn't be excluded just because of me.

Jessie nudged Rex in the side. "Look at the ass on that chick over there. Damn, even I'm a little into her."

"What?" Rex's head snapped so fast I almost heard a crack. "Where?" He suddenly turned back and glanced at Kayden before he looked away. "I mean...I've seen better."

Jessie narrowed her eyes at him. "Are you alright?"

I had to admit his behavior was peculiar, even to me. "You've seen better?" I took a glance at her. "No, Rex. You haven't."

Even Zeke checked her out. "If I weren't in a relationship, I'd ask for her number."

Rex shrugged then took a really long drink of his beer.

Kayden sipped her wine.

"I think…" Jessie continued to look at the woman on the other side of the bar. Her voice trailed away and her eyes expanded to the size of basketballs. "Uh…" She abandoned her drink on the counter then came to my side of the table. "Let's go to the bathroom."

"Why?" I didn't need to go, and last time I checked, we weren't in junior high.

"I need help with my makeup." She grabbed my wrist and tried to pull me away.

"Your makeup is perfect like always." I gently turned out of her grip and kept my place at the table. "Why are you being so weird right now?"

Rex glanced behind him then gave a similar reaction.

Kayden almost spilled her drink.

Zeke suddenly looked at his watch. "Damn, I didn't realize how late it was. We should get going."

It was ten.

Something was up.

I scanned the other side of the bar, and I immediately saw what they were trying to hide. Ryker moved through the crowd with his arm wrapped around the slender waist of a pretty brunette. He smiled down at her like he was having a great night out with a beautiful woman.

Rex bowed his head and closed his eyes. "Fuck."

Everything moved in slow motion as I watched them move together. I'd been the recipient of that smile so many times. He gave it to me just because he kissed me, usually in the corner of my mouth. I knew how that large and strong hand felt against my lower back. I remembered the way he would grip me tightly, like he never wanted to let go.

Two weeks apart and he was already picking up tail. And judging by the smile in his eyes, it wasn't his first time out. He'd been doing it for a while, maybe even before we officially broke up.

I couldn't stop staring even though the scene was absolutely horrifying. It broke my heart in a way it never had before. It shattered my belief that what we had was even real. He made love to me and I told him I loved him…and then he dumped me. It was the cruelest thing someone had ever done to me. And now he had already moved on with his life, hitting the sheets I used to sleep on almost every single night.

It hurt.

It really fucking hurt.

Ryker guided her forward and when his eyes moved for a gap in the crowd, they landed on mine.

He faltered in his movements because the surprise caught him off guard. He clearly thought there was no possibility of running into me because I'd be at home crying over him with an empty box of tissues beside me. For a moment, his eyes contained his guilt at being caught picking up someone new to fuck. But then he turned away and kept walking, his hand still around her waist. He moved past us and headed to the exit.

Everyone stood absolutely still and stared at me, unsure what I was going to do or say. I felt like a bomb they were trying to disarm. Any moment now, the wrong wire would be cut and I would implode.

There was no masking how much that hurt. Even now, I still loved him. I still dreamt about him. I still missed him. When he said he would never love me, he must have really meant it. Otherwise, he wouldn't be out having a good time right at that very moment.

Maybe I really did mean nothing to him.

"Excuse me." I grabbed my clutch and turned away from the table.

"Whoa, hold on." Zeke grabbed my wrist. "Rae, it's not worth it."

"If she wants to throw a drink in his face, she has every right," Jessie argued.

I tried to twist out of his grasp, but he was too strong.

"Rae, I'll gladly beat the shit out of him if you want. But don't confront him yourself." Zeke continued to pull me back.

"Let. Me. Go." I stared him down with fire in my eyes, ready to burn him with just a look.

Zeke gave me an angry look himself before he finally released me.

And I was off.

I walked out of the bar and reached the sidewalk. The freezing Seattle air hit me hard because I was practically wearing nothing. I was grateful Jessie made me look beautiful tonight. It was better than looking my worst while he walked out with an upgraded version of myself.

I spotted him walking to his car, his arm still around her waist.

I walked up to them, feeling my heart pound in my chest with spikes of adrenaline. I could hardly breathe because I was so anxious for what would happen next. I purposely waited until he got her in the passenger seat and shut the door before I made my move. This woman didn't know me. She probably didn't even know Ryker. So she didn't deserve my wrath. She was just an innocent person thinking she got lucky enough to find a man as beautiful as Ryker.

He turned around and stopped when he saw me. That same look of guilt was on his face, like he hated himself for doing what he just did. He rested his arms by his sides and kept his expression stoic. But his eyes still gave him away.

I wanted to scream.

I wanted to slap him.

I wanted to cry.

But I didn't do any of those things. I squared my shoulders, held my head high, and looked him square in the eye. With a steady voice filled with authority and power, I spoke calmly. "I feel sorry for you, Ryker."

His eyes softened because he hadn't expected me to lead with that.

"You see those guys?" I pointed to my friends who'd gathered on the sidewalk thirty feet away to witness the conversation.

Ryker glanced at them.

"I have people who love me. And I have people who I love. Ryker, you don't have anyone. You don't share your life with anyone. You don't share your secrets with a living soul. You're full of nothing but darkness and loneliness. I gave myself to you, I loved you because I thought there was something redeeming inside of you. But then the second something real happens, you get scared and run away. If that's how you want to live your life, then I feel so bad for you. Don't feel bad for me for breaking my heart. Feel bad for yourself for never having the honor of feeling love at all." I stared him down without blinking, my body still straight and graceful. I was a head shorter than him but I felt like a mountain. He hurt me. He shattered me. But I was still standing there. I was still breathing. I would have scars for a long time, but I still survived. "I'm going to find someone who's man enough to love a woman like me. I'm going to find a man fearless enough not to be afraid. And I can promise you, that man will never be you." I stepped away, still holding his gaze. "You made the biggest mistake of your life, Ryker. I can promise you that."

***

"That was awesome." Rex got the door unlocked and we all walked inside.

"It really was," Zeke said. "You put him in his place without even raising your voice."

"I bet he feels like shit." Jessie flipped her hair before she walked inside. "I doubt he could even get it up for her."

"That conversation will haunt him for the rest of his life," Kayden said. "If someone said that to me...I would have cried."

I appreciated the praise everyone gave me, and even though I was proud of myself for handling the situation the way I did, I didn't really feel better. My body didn't feel strong anymore. If anything, I felt weaker. The adrenaline had worn off and now all that was left was the cold truth. "Thanks, guys. I think I feel better because of it." That was a lie. But I wanted them to think I was okay so they would stop worrying about me. I didn't want them to know about this deep pit in my stomach that didn't seem to have a bottom. "I'm pretty tired. I think I'm going to hit the sack."

"Alright," Jessie said. "Me too." She turned to Kayden. "You want a ride?"

Kayden quickly glanced at Rex before she turned back to Jessie. "Yeah, sure."

"I guess I'm gonna take off too." Zeke walked up to me and raised his hand. "High five for that."

I smiled then slapped my palm against his.

"You're one badass woman." He pulled me in for a bear hug and gave me a tight squeeze. "No one messes with you." When he pulled away, he gave me an affectionate smile. "I'll see you tomorrow, alright?"

"Yeah, sure."

"Rochelle is coming over when I get home. I'm excited to tell her you're doing better. She's been worried."

"That's sweet of her." She was the sweetest girl Zeke had ever brought around. "Tell her I appreciate her concern."

"Absolutely." He patted me on the shoulder and walked out with everyone else.

I headed to bed with Safari and shut the door behind me. Once I was finally alone, I felt my knees go weak. I barely made it to the bed before I collapsed. My heels were uncomfortable so I slipped them off. I didn't bother taking off my dress because I didn't see the point.

I knew what was coming and there was no way to avoid it. Like an avalanche that could be heard before it was seen, the pain started deep in my chest. It slowly moved up my throat and into my eyes and my mouth.

One hot tear escaped, and I knew that was just the beginning.

I never cried if I could help it. It was a sign of weakness. It was an admission that I'd let someone get to me. But this time, I couldn't help it. When I saw him with that woman, I broke down. Despite the speech I gave, I was torn up inside. It hurt. It hurt so goddamn much.

I quieted my sobs so Rex wouldn't be able to hear me. The TV was on in the living room so he was probably watching something, the speakers muffling out all the noise I made.

Safari moved closer to me and rested his chin on my thigh. He looked up at me and whined, hurting inside because he knew I was hurting too.

I stroked my hand across his head and felt my tears fall on the bridge of his nose. "I'll be okay, Safari. I just need to let it out." I cried because I lost Ryker forever. I cried because he didn't give a damn about hurting me. I cried because I believed in a man who didn't deserve my faith. I cried because I gave him my entire heart—and he didn't want it.

One day, I would get better. But for now, I was heartbroken.

And I would be heartbroken for a long time.

The story continues in Book 3, Ray of Love.

Dear Reader,

Thank you for reading Ray of Hope. I hope you enjoyed reading it as much as I enjoyed writing it. If you could leave a short review, it would help me so much! Those reviews are the best kind of support you can give an author. Thank you!

Wishing you love,

E. L. Todd

Ray of Hope

E. L. Todd

Want To Stalk Me?

Subscribe to my newsletter for updates on new releases, giveaways, and for my comical monthly newsletter. You'll get all the dirt you need to know. Sign up today.

www.eltoddbooks.com

Facebook:

https://www.facebook.com/ELTodd42

Twitter:

@E_L_Todd

Now you have no reason not to stalk me. You better get on that.

Ray of Hope

I know I'm lucky enough to have super fans, you know, the kind that would dive off a cliff for you. They have my back through and through. They love my books, and they love spreading the word. Their biggest goal is to see me on the New York Times bestsellers list, and they'll stop at nothing to make it happen. While it's a lot of work, it's also a lot of fun. What better way to make friendships than to connect with people who love the same thing you do?

Are you one of these super fans?

If so, send a request to join the Facebook group. It's closed, so you'll have a hard time finding it without the link. Here it is:

https://www.facebook.com/groups/1192326920784373

Hope to see you there, ELITE!

Made in the USA
Lexington, KY
03 February 2017